# NORTHERN LIGHTS

LISE GOLD

*The northern cheek of the heavens,*
*By a sudden glory kissed,*
*Blushed to the tint of roses,*
*And hid in an amber mist,*
*And through the northern pathway,*
*Trailing her robe of flame,*
*The queenly Borealis*
*In her dazzling beauty came!*

— May Riley Smith, "Aurora Borealis"

# 1

## AN EVENING UNDER THE STARS

On the twenty-second of December 2017, Hannah Hudson and seven other tourists were gathered around a campfire in front of a small, privately-run, boutique hotel in the woods outside Kirkenes, Norway. The snow was pure, the air was crisply cold and the stars were bright, casting a faint glow over their surroundings. Hannah reached into her pocket for her phone, wanting to take a picture. The hotel – a traditional red wooden house with white windowsills – looked like a postcard scene, with candles and fairy lights in the windows and a Christmas tree on the generous front porch, next to a set of wooden rocking chairs. The six-bedroom hotel stood on the shore of a large lake that stretched out both long and wide in front of a mountain range. The lake was covered in ice and a smooth layer of thick snow, only broken up by tire tracks from the two four-wheel drives that had brought the hotel guests from the airport. Hannah could vaguely see the lines, dimly lit by the hotel's industrial spotlights, set up around the premises to keep the wolves away. Five rowing boats were beached upside down on the shore until spring, when the ice would melt and the lake would provide more than enough fish to feed the whole town. The tourists – three couples and two single women, one of which was Hannah – were speaking in low voices, as if afraid to disturb the peace around them. Legs stretched out in front of them, they were sitting back in their large army-style folding chairs, warming their toes after a long hike and sharing stories over hot chocolate with rum. Their red and white knitted blankets had been draped over their legs or shoulders at first, but now that the fire and the rum had warmed them, they used the blankets as pillows behind their backs to make themselves more comfortable as they rested their tired bodies from their first day out in the snow. Gunnar, a Danish pensioner, was already snoring, but his wife Sofia was wide awake, talking non-stop. Dinner had been simple: a thick, filling soup and homemade bread, also consumed around the campfire. Although the hotel had a nice dining area, dinner was going to be served outside under the stars most nights, unless there was snowfall – which reduced the chances of seeing the legendary northern lights significantly. But tonight the sky was clear and the stars were brighter than Hannah had ever seen them, and her travel companions were optimistic that this was the evening they would witness the elusive phenomenon. Their group consisted of Gunnar and Sofia, the couple from Denmark, Sarah and Joshua, newlyweds from Canada, Werner and his wife Charlotte from Germany, another married couple, and a woman on her own, who had introduced herself as Kristine Miller from the US. Everyone spoke English including Espen and his wife Dani, the hotel owners, who were also their tour guides for the duration of their five-night stay. Gunnar and Sofia were two culture-obsessed pensioners who spent most of their time traveling. After three years of visiting most of the USA and South America, they'd decided to try something a bit closer to home and so far, they hadn't been disappointed.

"I can hardly believe we're only an hour's flight from home," Sofia said, digging her heel into the snow as she attempted to create a star shape in front of her. "It seems a world away from Copenhagen." Sofia was restless and constantly fidgeting with something - a result of giving up smoking three months ago. She stretched and rolled her shoulders, shifting in her chair, then gently nudged Gunnar, who woke up and smiled at her.

"What's Copenhagen like?" Kristine, who was sitting next to Hannah, asked Sofia. "I'm going to spend New Year's Eve there. Flights back to the US were a lot cheaper from Denmark, so I thought I might as well."

"Oh, it's a lovely city but then it's our hometown so I might be biased." Sofia chuckled. "I've never met a tourist who wasn't charmed by it, though. I think you'll like it."

"It's marvelous," her husband Gunnar, chipped in. "Beautiful harbor, friendly people... it's got a small-town feel to it. We'll write down some must-see places for you to visit before you leave." He blinked a couple of times, fighting off the sleep.

"Thank you," Kristine said with a broad smile that had already caught Hannah's attention several times that day. "That's very nice of you. I like insiders' tips, they're always the best." She turned to Sarah, who was sitting opposite her. "What about you guys? Are you going elsewhere after this?"

"We are," Sarah said, beaming. "As we're in Europe already, we're going to visit Paris and Rome before we head back to Canada. But this is the highlight of our trip, for sure. It's always been our dream to see the northern lights, hasn't it, Josh?"

Josh, her husband, nodded. "Yes. Sarah's been talking about it for years, how she'd love to come here. So, we decided to wait for a couple of months instead of going on our honeymoon straight after the wedding. We wanted to be here during the northern lights season to broaden our chances of seeing it but also to get the full experience with the snow. It's quite something isn't it?" He looked at his watch. "I just can't get used to the lack of light, though. My body constantly thinks it's time to go to sleep and I feel really tired."

"I know. I'm getting used to it now but I felt the same yesterday," Kristine said. "The perpetual dark is strange. I feel like I'll be spending my days waiting for the sun to come up."

"It feels unnatural," Werner agreed. "Yet, there's nothing unnatural about it." They all continued chatting for a while about their previous travels and about their expectations for the rest of the week.

"How is everyone doing?" Espen asked as he joined the group, looking up at the star-studded sky with his big hands buried deep in the pockets of his padded navy snowsuit. Underneath he was wearing a gray hand-knitted sweater with a traditional Norwegian pattern. With his broad shoulders, his thick blonde hair and a healthy blush on his cheeks, Espen was a picture-perfect Scandinavian.

"I love it here," Kristine answered. "It's even more beautiful than I expected."

"Absolutely loving it," Sofia said.

"Great." Espen fished a small tin box out of his pocket, took out a bag of snus, and popped it under his upper lip. It made his mouth gape in a funny way. "It's just tobacco," he explained when he saw his guests' confused stares. "Anyone want to try some?" He held out the box before them.

"Thank you, why not?" Joshua said taking what looked like a small tea bag out of the box, eager to give it a try as the rest looked on warily. He gingerly put the pouch in between his upper lip and his teeth and looked around the circle with a slightly gaping mouth.

"You look ridiculous, Josh." Sarah grimaced at his comical expression. "Why?" she asked Espen. "What's so nice about it? Surely it must taste disgusting." She turned back to Joshua. "I'm not kissing you tonight, as long as you know that."

Espen laughed and shrugged. "There's no reason for popping snus, just like there's no reason for smoking. It gives an instant nicotine hit though, I like that. My grandfather did it and my father did it too. I guess it was hard to buy cigarettes in the middle of winter back then." He pointed at the tire tracks on the frozen lake. "It still is, so I hope there are no smokers amongst you without a stash to last you five days. If you get desperate have some of this, it takes the cravings away. I tried it for the first time when I was fifteen, and it made me feel energized on my long walks to school in the mornings, so I kept on using it." He shrugged. "And now, I can't stop, despite Dani's daily pleas. She thinks it's disgusting."

"I think I might agree with that," Josh said with the bag in his mouth. "It makes me talk funny too." There were some giggles at his mumbling.

"Doesn't look like we're going to see the lights tonight," Espen said, turning his attention back to the sky. He had made sure everyone's expectations were realistic. "Northern lights, or aurora borealis as we call them, are not something we can guarantee you'll see during your stay, and I don't want you to be disappointed if they don't appear," he had said when they arrived that morning. "There's so much more our fantastic country has to offer. Being here in the wild is a once-in-a-lifetime experience for most people. My wife Dani and I will do everything we can to make your stay memorable and I have no doubt you will have an amazing time here in Kirkenes, whether you get to see the northern lights or not."

The group had mumbled their understanding, still standoffish as they hadn't gotten to know each other properly yet. But apparently a four-hour long hike, during today's only hours of dim twilight, was all it had taken to make people bond. To everyone's excitement, they'd seen a wolf, fresh bear prints, and the most stunning and otherworldly views, and that alone would give them enough to talk about for the weeks to come.

"How can you tell when the lights will appear and when they won't?" Kristine asked.

Espen frowned as he studied the stars, two deep furrows appearing between his eyebrows. "I've been living here my whole life," he mumbled, hard to understand with the pouch of tobacco settled underneath his lip. "I recognize the signs but it's hard to explain to someone who's never seen them before. It's like there's an electric charge in the air. There are these tiny little sparks, almost invisible to the naked eye, before the light appears." He looked at his watch. "It's almost eleven now, I really don't think it's going to happen. The lights usually appear between 9pm and 1am, but feel free to stay out all night if you want, you never know. We don't lock the doors around here." He smiled as he turned and walked back to the hotel. "Just don't leave it open, we don't want a family of bears raiding the kitchen." He stopped, glanced up one more time and sighed. "Well, maybe tomorrow."

. . .

HANNAH LOOKED out over the snow-covered lake. She felt a good kind of tired but her body was also confused at the lack of daylight. The sun never came up in December and living in vague twilight for only four hours a day was something she'd never experienced before. Her muscles were aching and it was nice to sit slumped in her chair, warmed by the fire. The feeling in her feet was starting to come back and for the first time in a long while, she felt carefree. Stressful thoughts of her busy restaurant in London had faded to the background. She trusted her staff, and anyway, so what if something went wrong? It wasn't like she could beam herself back there. She was in the middle of nowhere, without a direct connection to London, and the flights to Oslo only went twice a week. The Wi-Fi signal was weak and she'd already stopped trying to send messages hours ago. Kristine had not given up yet, holding her phone in the air every once in a while, checking to see if it had sparked into life. Hannah and Kristine had only spoken to each other briefly on their walk today because Kristine had, possibly against her will, been ambushed by the Canadian couple who had jumped on her as soon as they'd heard her American accent. Why they were so delighted to meet an American on their holiday in Norway was beyond Hannah, but she'd left them alone after that, and walked on with the two German high-school teachers and the Danish pensioners, who had been surprisingly good company.

"No luck?" she asked, turning to Kristine when she lifted her phone up again.

"Nothing." Kristine gave her a smile. "It's not important. I'm just addicted to my phone, I guess. I never realized it until now."

"I gave up late this afternoon," Hannah said. "I haven't

checked it since, apart from using my camera. It feels kind of liberating. You should try it."

Kristine demonstratively put her phone in the brown leather satchel between her feet and closed the straps.

"There," she said. "You're right. So... what do we do now? Talk? Socialize? I'm not sure I remember how to do that." She laughed.

"Don't worry. I'm sure we can come up with a subject that will absorb you enough to stop you reaching for your bag every five minutes." Hannah studied Kristine's face. She was pretty, with big blue eyes, a healthy tan and long blonde hair with a natural wave that cascaded down her shoulders. Perhaps that was the reason, Hannah thought, however shallow, that she had wanted to talk to her so badly today. "Are you enjoying yourself?" she asked. "I couldn't help but notice we're the only two people in the group that have come out here on our own."

"Yeah. I'm having a great time," Kristine said with a slight Southern twang. "How about you? Were you nervous, coming here by yourself?" Her lips pulled into a huge smile when she sat forward, leaning her elbows on her knees as she turned to Hannah. "Because I'm not going to lie, I was shitting myself."

"No, not nervous per se," Hannah said, amused by Kristine's dramatics. "But I expected to be all by myself and I was fine with that." She looked around the group who, apart from Gunnar, who was fast asleep again, were getting tipsier and louder by the second. "I never expected it to be this sociable."

"Yeah. They seem like a nice bunch, don't they?" Kristine looked Hannah up and down, then let her eyes linger on her lips. "So, why did you come here?" she asked. "Was it the northern lights that drew you?"

"No, not really." Hannah sat back and tucked her blanket behind her head. "I just haven't had a holiday in years and I really needed to get away from everything for a bit. I have a restaurant in London and as you can probably imagine, it's next to impossible to get away for more than a couple of days at a time. So I thought Norway would be perfect for a short break. Besides the relatively short flight, I was hoping I could really switch off here. When I'm traveling, I tend to spend most of my time exploring the local food; what I like about it, what I don't like about it, how I can take inspiration from the food culture for my own menu, and so on. My mind never stops." She shot a quick glance at the hotel, making sure Espen was out of sight. "I heard Norway has one of the least exciting cuisines in the world, at least out here in the sticks. And I knew it would be quiet. Thought I might get some proper rest. Escaping the Christmas madness in London is a bonus. And guess what?" She grinned. "I was right. This is great. It's quiet, there are no commercial establishments that have anything to do with food or drink, or anything else for that matter, and now I have no phone signal so I can't stress over my restaurant."

"Good for you," Kristine said, nudging her. "You must be the only person here not obsessing over a sighting of the northern lights, then."

"So that's why you're here?" Hannah asked. "All the way from the US? Which state are you from?"

"I'm from the South," Kristine said. "Louisiana. I live in a small town called Covington." Sarah, who was sitting next to Kristine, passed her the rum and Kristine topped up her hot chocolate and passed it on to Hannah. "Nice system they've got going here with the rum. I think I like these Norwegians." She giggled. "But to get back to why I'm here, all I can say is that I get terribly curious about distant, exotic locations. So when I read about this nearly magical natural spectacle, I just had to come and see it." She shrugged. "Or not. It doesn't really matter, I'm beyond excited already. Can you believe we saw a wolf today?" She gestured towards the landscape around them. "And this part of the world is amazing. Have you ever seen so much snow in your life?"

"No, I don't think I have." Hannah laughed, looking out over the forest and the lake. It was a beautiful sight. Bright white, thick layers of fluffy snow stretched out in front of her. Apart from the spotlights, the land was lit by the starry sky and the moon, its light casting an eerie glow over the surface of the snow, giving it a bluish undertone. "I'd be terrified if I was here on my own," she said, shivering.

"Me too." Kristine shuffled her chair a little closer to Hannah, clearly keen to keep the conversation going. "I hope I'll be able to sleep tonight. I didn't notice how quiet it was yesterday as I was too exhausted from my journey. Even though I'm from a small town myself, this is a whole different level of quiet out here. It's as if the snow is absorbing all the sound somehow."

"You're right." Hannah listened intently. She heard talking and the cracking of the logs on the fire but, apart from that, the silence was so deep, it was almost palpable. "It's kind of creepy, don't you think? Maybe we should share a room," she joked.

Kristine laughed. "I'll come and find you if I freak out tonight." She had a great laugh, Hannah thought. And a great face. High cheekbones, those electric blue eyes, great teeth and of course that thick, long, sun-bleached blonde hair. Hannah's eyes shifted down. *Banging body too.* Although it was hard to make out any shape under the thick checked flannel shirt Kristine was wearing, Hannah had already taken her in over breakfast that morning, unconsciously focusing on the only other single woman in their group. But there was also something else that she'd picked up on during her brief conversation with Kristine. She had a faint suspicion Kristine might be gay. Although she didn't display any of the stereotypical signs, she'd given Hannah a curious glance-over when they'd first introduced themselves, as if she was trying to figure her out. Hannah knew it might just be wishful thinking but she couldn't resist digging further.

"Are you single?" Hannah heard herself ask. Then she frantically shook her head and laughed. "I didn't mean in relation to sharing a room. God, I totally sound like I'm preying on you now, but I promise I'm not. I'm just curious."

Kristine gave her an intense look, causing Hannah's heart to skip a beat. "Yes." She chuckled. "I'm single. Covington isn't exactly the best place to meet women." She paused; making sure her point had come across. "What about you?"

Hannah smiled. "Super single." She felt a jolt of excitement at Kristine's comment. *Thank Christ my gaydar is still working.* Although she hadn't come here to make friends or to meet women, having a single lesbian in their group was most definitely an exciting distraction, especially one as attractive as Kristine.

"You say that as if it's a blessing," Kristine remarked.

"Yeah well, my ex, she kind of fucked me over, so right now I'm just enjoying life as a single woman in London." Hannah shrugged. "We were together for ten years, Beth and I, and we even worked together. But I'm over the worst heartache. Let's just say I'm having as much fun as I possibly can and I have no intention of committing myself to anyone anytime soon."

"I have no doubt you get around." Kristine studied

Hannah with renewed interest. "You're cute. But cool-cute, you know? London-cool-cute. Have you ever tried Tinder or that She-app?" She picked up her bag to grab her phone, then remembered she wouldn't have a signal and dropped it back. "Never mind. I forgot it doesn't work here."

"No, I'm not on Tinder," Hannah said with a giggle. "There are more than enough single lesbians in London and lots of club nights where I can hook up. Not to mention the straight women who all seem desperate to experiment lately. It's become a bit of a trend after all those actresses, models and singers came out last year. I haven't really needed those apps yet, but maybe in the future, who knows?" She leaned closer to Kristine and lowered her voice to make sure their conversation stayed private. "How do you meet women, down South in the US? Surely that can't be easy."

"I don't." Kristine sighed. "My friends try to set me up sometimes but it's never worked out. They were all great women, don't get me wrong, but I wasn't attracted to them. I mean, I don't want to date someone just because they happen to be gay and live reasonably close. That makes no sense. I want it all, you know. The attraction, the sparks..." She rolled her eyes. "Listen to me; I'm pouring my heart out already. I think the holiday excitement might be getting to me. More rum?" she asked, passing Hannah the bottle.

"Sure. I never say no." Hannah happily refilled her mug with rum and hot chocolate from the large thermos in between them. She then held up her mug and clinked it with Kristine's before taking a sip. "So, you don't mind spending Christmas away from home?"

"Well, it's not ideal." Kristine paused. "My parents were a bit hurt that I won't be with them for Christmas, but this was the only time I could get off work and I really wanted to go on this trip. But I have to say, even by myself, I'm feeling the Christmas spirit here. The music playing inside, the snow, the decorations and the smell of cinnamon everywhere... I don't think Christmas could be more perfect if I'd designed it myself. I spent two nights in Oslo before I flew here, so my jetlag could settle, and then arrived here. After Christmas I'm going to Copenhagen for five nights, so I'll be there on New Year's Eve. Thought I might as well make the most of it while I'm in Scandinavia." She took a sip of her drink. "What about you?"

"You mean how do I feel about spending Christmas on my own?" Hannah shrugged. "I'm just happy to be out of London during the busiest time of the year. To be honest, I'm not in contact with my family, so I usually spend the week working my ass off to give my staff Christmas Eve, Christmas Day, or Boxing Day off. I've never really cared about the December festivities, always thought they were overrated. But I have to agree that there's something very charming about being here." She tried to suppress a yawn but failed.

Kristine started yawning too. "I think the day is catching up with me too," she said. "I hope I'll be able to get out of this chair, my legs are killing me after that hike."

"Want some help getting up? I'm going to bed anyway." Hannah stood up and held out her hand.

"Thank you." Kristine shot her a sweet smile. "But I think I'll stay out here for a little while longer. It's such a perfect night. Besides, I'm still hoping to catch a glimpse of those lights." That wasn't entirely true. Kristine was exhausted, but she didn't want Hannah to think she was following her around, desperately hoping for some action, so she sank deeper into her chair and waved at Hannah. "Sleep well, Hannah. Come and find me if you get scared."

"Sweet dreams, Kristine. I will." Hannah laughed and winked at Kristine before she turned to the rest of the group. "Goodnight everyone. Today was fun."

KRISTINE WATCHED Hannah walk back towards the hotel. She was so different to the women she'd met back home. She wasn't trying to impress her and she wasn't trying to be someone she wasn't. She was just simply herself, in a relaxed and confident way. Kristine was sure that if they'd met in any other place, she would have ignored Hannah, too intimidated by her appearance to engage her in conversation. Even Hannah's walk was cool, the way she swung her arms casually, holding her back straight even when she walked uphill, never in a hurry. But she hadn't been intimidating at all. In fact, Hannah seemed like a really nice person and Kristine felt curiously drawn to her now. She was attractive, with a delicate bone structure, pale skin, a carefully styled dark 'messy' bob, that was always covered by a beanie, and had big, sharp brown, eyes underneath shapely eyebrows that had a glint of steel in them. Those eyes had captured Kristine's attention the first time she'd looked into them and so had the tattoo on her neck that just peeked out above the neckline of her sweater. And then there was her cute smile, pulling slightly to the left, and of course her British accent, which was practically catnip to most Americans. Hannah wouldn't be Kristine's type normally but that was only because she'd never met anyone like her. She felt a flutter in her belly at the thought they'd be stuck here together for the coming days. It had been a long time since she'd been instantly attracted to someone. She shook her head and dismissed her fantasy as silly. Why would Hannah be attracted to a simple country girl like her?

She seemed way too complex for that. Not damaged-goods complex, that wasn't the vibe Kristine was getting from her. Just different. She waited until Hannah was out of sight, then stood up to go to her room too.

"Goodnight folks," she said, giving the group a wave. "I'm going to bed. I'll see y'all tomorrow."

Kristine took off her boots in the hallway and walked through the open living and dining room area, where two generous beige corduroy three-seater couches, and a smaller corner couch, were placed around the big fireplace that had been burning for hours, leaving black marks on the floor where the ash had flicked over the hearth's front edge. The drapes looked home-made, not because they were sloppy, but because the red and white checked fabric suited the lake facing windows so perfectly in style and size that they looked like they'd been made with love. The tables in the dining area were made of timber and had red table-cloths on them, matching the red cushions on the dining chairs. The walls and floor were lined with timber too, along with the staircase and even the bathroom. The interior of the hotel couldn't have looked more Scandinavian, with the thick rugs on the floors and local artwork on the walls, showcasing mythical creatures and snow scenes. Upstairs was a sauna for community use. Kristine had never been in a sauna before and decided she'd use it at her earliest opportunity. But right now, she was too tired to venture anywhere but her bed. Her bedroom was tastefully decorated, with sliding doors to a big balcony with a view to die for. She closed the door to her room and searched for the switch that connected the lights to the Christmas tree in the corner. Seeing the twinkling white lights illuminate immediately triggered the Christmas spirit in her. Espen and Dani had put a lot of effort into creating a welcoming Christmas atmosphere. She lit the candles in the reindeer candleholders on her nightstand, then filled a glass with ice cold water from the tap in her bathroom and drank the whole lot, hoping she wouldn't have a headache in the morning from all the rum she'd consumed. Kristine started stripping off her three layers of clothing. She began by removing her thick red and black checked flannel shirt that she often used as a jacket in winter. Then the padded snowsuit provided by the hotel, along with a pair of black thermal leggings and finally a tight black brushed fleece top. It had been more than enough to keep her warm during the hike and the cold night but now she felt strangely naked, standing there in only a black lingerie set. Having been single for so long, she didn't really bother with nice matching underwear anymore, but just in case, she'd bought a couple of sets for her trip. Her visit to a lesbian bar in Oslo when she'd first arrived in Norway had been a complete disaster. Kristine wasn't used to being in busy, public places by herself. Despite her jetlag she'd summoned all her courage and had dressed up in jeans and a new top, hoping to meet some nice people, but once there, she was overcome with social anxiety. The establishment was friendly but she'd felt awkward on her own in a place where everyone seemed to know each other. After downing two glasses of wine in ten minutes, she'd fled the scene, disappointed with herself but also relieved to be back in the safety of her own hotel room. Maybe she was too used to the comfort of her own small town, where she knew everyone. Maybe she was just a coward. Or maybe she'd simply forgotten how to talk to new people. But she'd talked to her fellow group members today, and to Hannah, a woman who had captured her attention from the moment she'd arrived at the airport. They hadn't spoken much then, as they'd been driven to the hotel in separate cars. But she'd made up for it tonight and it had been really great talking to her. Encouraged by the rum in her system, Kristine had been outgoing and honest. She was proud that she'd finally been able to hold a decent conversation with a beautiful woman. Hannah was surprisingly easy to talk to, despite having that typical London attitude about her. Her thin frame, paired with the brisk way she walked, hadn't gone unnoticed by Kristine. Hannah looked like someone who was used to being on her feet all day. She had aced the hike like a walk in the park. While others had been resting on tree trunks every twenty minutes, catching their breath, Hannah had been running around taking pictures and feeding squirrels from the bag of nuts she'd brought with her. Kristine wondered how Hannah dressed when she was at home in London. Here at the hotel, everyone arrived at breakfast in their thermal leggings, woolen socks provided by the hotel, and thick sweaters or cable knit jumpers. It was like wearing uniforms at boarding school.

Kristine switched on the kettle on the bureau to make herself a cup of cinnamon tea and opened the tin of homemade cookies that Dani had left in all the rooms as a welcome present. *'Pepperkaker'*, it said on the Christmas label on the side of the tin. The delicious aroma of cinnamon and cardamom slowly spread across the room. She poured the hot water into one of the red mugs next to the kettle, dipped her teabag several times, took a bite of one of the star-shaped cookies and closed her eyes in delight. It was really good. *I bet Hannah is analyzing the cookies right now, trying to work out the ingredients.* She smiled at that. There was no doubt that Kristine was fascinated by the gorgeous Brit, who talked in that beautiful, pure accent she'd only ever heard on TV. She wondered if Hannah would even have given her a second glance if they'd met anywhere else, except a hotel in the middle of nowhere. *Probably not.* She picked up her mug, walked over to the full-length mirror and took a sip of her tea, staring at her own reflection. She usually worked in her vegetable patch on weekends and sometimes after work, making up in physical activity for the many hours she spent behind her desk in her office at the bank during the week. Her arms and legs were tanned from the long hours in the blazing Southern sun. She looked good though for thirty-five and all the hard work outside in the fresh air had kept her in shape. She turned around and checked out her ass in the skimpy panties that barely covered half of it. *Not bad.*

After a long shower, Kristine put on the fluffy white robe that the hotel had provided and slipped into a pair of equally fluffy slippers with '*God Jul*' embroidered on them. That was Norwegian for '*Merry Christmas*', she'd learned by now. Then she got her phone out of her bag and attempted to send another message to Carol-Anne, her neighbor, who had promised to water her crops while she was away. This time the message was sent successfully, and she did a little victory dance on the rug, relieved that she'd been able to get through. Her yard was the only thing Kristine worried about, and although Carol-Anne was one of the sweetest people she knew, unfortunately, her forgetfulness more than matched her sweetness. Kristine's beloved dog Belle would be fine; as she was staying with her brother for the twelve days she was away. She was sure Belle would be spoilt rotten with leftovers from Christmas dinner and long walks in the fields along her brother's farm. She wasn't worried about her job either. She'd appointed Mary, the accounts manager, to be interim general manager in her absence. Mary was competent and would manage just fine. But her vegetable patch needed looking after, especially with the drought predicted for this month. She glanced over at the phone on her nightstand and felt the urge to call her neighbor, just in case she didn't check her mobile phone. It was earlier in the US, so it wasn't like she would wake her up, and after five days from home she longed to hear a familiar voice. She looked up Carol-Anne's number on her mobile and dialed it.

"Hello?" a thin voice said.

"Hey Carol-Anne, it's Kristine. How are you?"

"Kristine?" Carol-Anne sounded surprised.

"Yeah, it's me. How are you? And how are the veggies doing? Have you been watering them?"

"Of course I have, sweetheart. I'm taking care of them as if they were my own babies. Your leeks look like they're ready. Want me to take them out?"

"Sure," Kristine said. "Please take and use whatever you like. They're just going to rot if you keep them for me. And thank you. You know how much I worry about my yard."

"It's my pleasure," Carol-Anne said in a cracked voice. "How's Sweden?"

"Norway," Kristine corrected her.

"Of course, I remember now." Carol-Anne chuckled. "I still wouldn't be able to point it out on the map if I had a gun to my head, so forgive me."

"It's fine." Kristine laughed. "It's amazing here. It's dark all day. There's just a hint of twilight between eleven and three in the afternoon but that's about it. The stars and the moon are all the light we have, and everything's covered in snow. It's breathtaking."

"What? Dark all day did you say? Sounds pretty darn depressing if you ask me. But interesting nevertheless. Be careful, will you? I bet there's a whole bunch of wild animals out there, hungry for a tasty spring chicken like you."

"I'll be careful," Kristine said. "Thanks Carol-Anne. I

won't keep you any longer. I just wanted to check in, that's all."

"Thank you for calling. Now you take care, sweetheart. I spoke to Jason today, your colleague at the bank. They all miss you down there."

"That's sweet. Tell them I miss them too if you see them again," Kristine lied.

"I will, darling. Take care now."

Kristine reflected on her colleagues after she'd hung up. She certainly didn't miss them. They were nice, sure, but she couldn't say she considered any of them as friends. They weren't her type of people. She couldn't see herself having a casual drink with them, the way she had with the people in her group tonight. There was always some small talk on Monday morning but the reply to the 'how-was-your-weekend' question was always the same: dinner with the parents or in-laws on Saturdays unless there was an anniversary or a birthday. Special occasions in Covington were generally celebrated at Romeo's, an Italian restaurant. It was also the only restaurant in town that had real candles on the tables, which apparently equaled romance to even the most burnt-out of marriages. Then there was church on Sundays and sometimes something about the kids' sports games or birthday parties. Not that Kristine had much to contribute to general chit-chat. She worked in her yard, read a lot and took the occasional trip to New Orleans to see her best friend Kate, who had moved there for her job three years ago. All in all, she had nothing in common with her colleagues and quite frankly, she didn't mind that at all. Finance wasn't Kristine's passion, growing things was. But the job paid the bills and allowed her to travel wherever she wanted, provided she could get the time off. She'd never been very ambitious but she was more than competent at her job and good at managing people. She'd been promoted to general manager at the local bank at a rather young age, perhaps because her colleagues weren't up to the job, or perhaps because the bosses had recognized her natural talent for strategic planning and generating commercial growth. Anyway, she never minded going into work but she wasn't necessarily looking forward to going back either. She'd been there ten years now. Another year, another twelve months of going into the same office, doing the same things, loomed ahead of her. Another year of most likely being single, unable to meet women she connected with in the area where she lived. Nothing ever changed in Covington and nothing ever changed in her life. She'd told herself many times she had nothing to complain about. No one was forcing her to stay but she had no reason to move elsewhere either. That was why she loved to travel. It was a way of escaping her boring life, even if only for a little while. Kristine didn't mind traveling on her own, it made her feel brave and free, even though it wasn't always plain sailing.

Kristine pondered whether to send her mother a message, taking advantage of the fact that she still had reception. Just like Carol-Anne, her mother was one those people who rarely checked their messages. Nine out of ten times she never even saw them, and she certainly wouldn't know how to reply, even though Kristine had explained the workings of her simple cell phone over and over again. Still, she decided to send one after all, just to make herself feel better about the fact that she wouldn't be there for Christmas.

*Hi Mom, just letting you know that I'm fine and having a good time. Reception is bad here, so just in case I don't get the chance to call you in the coming days, I want to wish you and*

*Dad a great Christmas and a nice time with the family. Thinking of you. Kristine X.*

Kristine smiled to herself. There was never anything nice about their family get-togethers. For some reason there was always a fight over dinner, no matter how small or insignificant the reason. Her two brothers, Joe and Jed, didn't get along at all. Her father was as stubborn as a mule and still in denial about the fact that Kristine was gay. She put her phone down and sighed as she fell down on her bed, exhausted but happy. At least she wouldn't have to put up with the drama this Christmas.

## 2

## THE SAUNA

Steam was rising up from the sizzling hot stones when Hannah threw water on them. She sat down and leaned back against the third wooden step in the sauna. It was nice to wake up like this and she wondered why she hadn't thought of it sooner. Twenty minutes sitting here, and a cold shower after, would be enough to give her that little extra boost of energy she needed to be sociable over breakfast. That and she was kind of hoping that Kristine might have the same idea. She closed her eyes and tried to relax but Kristine's smile and her big, blue eyes kept appearing before her. Hannah had found Kristine attractive the first time they'd met but she'd put it down to that old adage – 'availability is the mother of attraction'. A little flirting was one thing, there was nothing wrong with that. But now she was actively thinking of her even though she wasn't around and that was strange. She'd told herself that she was here to rest. Of course Kristine was attractive, especially in this context; compared to the straight, middle-aged couples she was surrounded by. She wasn't going to let herself get carried away by something that was only in her head and make a mountain out of a molehill. Yet here she was, all hot and bothered, hoping that Kristine would walk in any minute, with only a towel covering her very sexy body and having all sorts of inappropriate thoughts at what she wanted to do to that luscious body. Her eyes shot open when the door handle turned. *Please let it be Kristine.* But she wasn't that lucky today.

"Good morning Hannah." A very chirpy Werner stomped in and closed the door behind him. His tiny towel was tied low under his big belly, barely covering enough to pass for decent. The knowledge he was most likely wearing nothing underneath made it almost painful to face him. He'd shaven his chest, she noted in surprise, seeing the shave-cuts on his pale skin as he sat down opposite her. It looked painful.

"Morning Werner. How are you today?" she asked, frantically thinking of topics to discuss if she was going to spend the next fifteen minutes here alone with him.

"I'm excellent, thank you. Had a nice sleep, woke up fresh despite the rum..." he paused and winked for extra effect. "Thought I'd try the sauna. Charlotte doesn't like saunas. She says they're too hot. I said to her that's the whole point of a sauna, *liebchen*, but no. She said she'd rather spend the extra half hour in bed." *Oh no, he's in a talking mood and I haven't even had my first coffee yet.* His bald head was sweating already and his chubby cheeks were red from the heat.

"I get that," Hannah tried. "It's much harder to wake up here, without the daylight."

"Well I've never had a problem with waking up since I joined the Marines in nineteen seventy-nine. They made us get up at four every morning and it ruined my sleep pattern." He leaned forward and spread his legs apart, resting his elbows on his thighs as drops of sweat fell down from his chin. Hannah kept her eyes firmly fixed on his face, not wavering for fear of seeing something she couldn't make unseen. He hadn't done it on purpose, she knew that. Werner didn't strike her as a flasher, but still, it wasn't something she was willing to be confronted with at this time of day, or any day for that matter. She grinned at that thought and made a mental note to tell Kristine about it. At least Werner was easy to talk to. All she had to do was ask a question and she could zone out and pretend to listen until she'd stayed long enough to leave without seeming impolite.

"So… the Marines. That must have been an exciting time. Where were you stationed?" she asked.

## 3

## BREAKFAST

"Hey Hannah." Kristine sat down opposite Hannah in the dining room where breakfast was being served.

"Good morning," Hannah said, coating her two heart-shaped hot buttermilk waffles with homemade jelly. They were really, really good. But they weren't so good as to account for the sheepish grin that had spread across her face. That was Kristine's presence, she realized. Her heart started thumping in her throat when Kristine's button-down cardigan fell open, revealing a hint of cleavage under her low-cut t-shirt. She pulled her gaze from the full breasts and forced herself to look Kristine in the eyes. "Did you manage to sleep?"

"Like a baby." Kristine put her coffee mug down and slowly buttered her toast, still waking up. "You?"

"Fantastic," Hannah said. "I managed to drag myself out of bed and went to the sauna first thing but I'm still tired. I think it's my body telling me it's the middle of the night, even though it's ten in the morning." She gestured at the windows. It was dark outside, the kind of dark she would expect to see at 2am in London. "But I figured I'd be missing out on so much if I stayed here by myself all day, so that got me going. Are you going on the husky ride?"

"Of course." Kristine took a sip of her coffee, winced, added more sugar and took another sip. "It's always been a dream of mine and I still can't believe it's actually going to happen today." She fell silent for a moment. "Hey, do you want to share a sled with me? I don't mind going alone but it will be more fun together, right?"

"Sure. I'd love to." Hannah tried to ignore the flutter in her stomach at the thought of having Kristine sitting between her legs and having a legitimate reason to put her arms around her waist. *Jesus. Why can't I just manage one week without trying to get into someone's pants?* "Have you tried these waffles?" she asked, trying to steer her mind away from indecent thoughts revolving around groping Kristine on a sled. "They're so good. And this blueberry jam, or as you American's say 'jelly', is to die for. I need to ask Dani for the recipe."

"You're doing the exact thing you said you were trying to avoid." Kristine laughed. "But if it's that good... can I try some?"

"Of course." *Does she want to use my fork?* Hannah looked at Kristine, trying to read her. Kristine made no attempt to help herself, so she speared her fork through a piece of waffle and held it in front of Kristine's full, peach colored lips. They pulled into a smile when Kristine reached out and folded her slender fingers around Hannah's wrist before she took the bite off her fork. She closed her eyes and moaned, holding on to Hannah's wrist for just a little longer than necessary. Her grip did something to Hannah, something she hadn't felt in a long time. The spark didn't subside when Kristine let go and leaned back in her seat.

"Mmm... So good. I might have to get some of those." Kristine's lips glistened with the sugary jelly.

Hannah found herself staring at her mouth. If she wasn't mistaken, Kristine was flirting with her. She shifted in her seat, unsure whether to flirt back or not. *Come on, Hannah. You're not one to shy away from a bit of flirtation. Say something. Something funny.*

"I never asked you what you do for a living," she said, disappointed with her lame question. She did want to know though. She was genuinely interested in Kristine's life and she'd beaten herself up over the fact that she hadn't asked more questions the previous night.

"My job is boring compared to yours." Kristine used a cheese slicer to cut a piece of cheesy substance off a mysterious brown block before placing it on her toast.

"Come on, I'm sure it's not that bad. Tell me." Hannah was eyeing the brown block that Kristine seemed surprisingly familiar with, mystified as to what it was.

"I'm the general manager of a bank," Kristine said. "See? Boring." She laughed. "I like my job but there's absolutely nothing about it that would be interesting to discuss socially."

"That's nonsense." Hannah shifted in her seat at the vision of Kristine behind a desk, wondering why the hell the idea was so arousing. "So, do you have an office? Do you wear a suit to work? High heels?" She gave Kristine a smirk.

"Yes, I have an office and twelve people working for me. It's only a small local branch but we do well. And yes, I do wear a suit." Kristine laughed. "And heels. Why do you ask? That's an unusual question."

Hannah shrugged. "I've always had a thing for suits." She felt her cheeks flush. "By the way, what's that you're eating?"

Kristine looked up at her and held her gaze with an amused smile. "Changing the subject now, are we?" She handed Hannah her piece of toast. "It's Norwegian goat's cheese. They don't export it, that's why you've never seen it before. I tried it in Oslo, before I came here."

Hannah took a bite from the cheesy toast and handed it back to Kristine. "Strange," she said. "But good strange. There's a hint of goat but also something sweet... is it caramel? And why is it brown?" She took the block of cheese and cut off another slice, then put it in her mouth, slowly chewing while trying to work out the ingredients.

"No idea. Could be?" Kristine paused. "I get what you meant now, when you said you became obsessive over food when you traveled. It's really cute." Then she put a hand in front of her mouth, suppressing a chuckle. "I didn't mean that, I..." She stopped halfway through her sentence. "God, it must be the lack of light here. It's making me all weird and giddy."

"I can't say I mind if it makes you think I'm cute." Hannah grinned. Although she was fully blushing now, she didn't shy away from accepting the compliment.

Kristine looked like she'd been thrown off her game and stood up abruptly. She walked over to the breakfast buffet and helped herself to some waffles and blueberry jelly. Hannah watched her linger there much longer than necessary, doing nothing in particular. By the time she returned to their table, she'd composed herself.

"Subject closed," she said. "It's too early for this kind of talk before I've finished my first coffee." A small smile played around her mouth.

"Morning guys. Is everything okay?" Dani interrupted them.

"It's all great, thank you." Hannah looked up at their tall

hostess with her long, blonde hair. Dani was about her age, she guessed. Early thirties, certainly not older. "Your jam is the best I've ever tasted. I'd love to have your recipe." She hesitated. "Unless it's a secret?"

Dani laughed. "Nothing secret about it. Just blueberries and sugar. We have great blueberries here in late summer, so you can't really go wrong. We do try to make as much as we can when we have the chance, so we have a stash for the winter months. Almost everything here is home-made or locally sourced. It's quite a hassle to drive to the nearest supermarket, especially in winter." She brightened. "Anyway, I like to keep it simple, let the ingredients speak for themselves."

"Simple is good." Hannah said. "And I don't think I've had a decent cup of old-fashioned filter coffee in years. I forgot how good it is."

"I'm glad you like it." Dani looked from Hannah to Kristine and back. "Are you guys excited for the husky ride?"

Kristine nodded her enthusiasm before swallowing her last piece of waffle. "Absolutely. I can't wait."

"It's great fun. I'm always looking forward to it myself," Dani said. "In case you were worried about the dogs, you need to know that they have a great life and they love going out with the sleds, so you don't need to feel sorry for them," she assured them. "Some people are apprehensive about it because they think it puts a strain on the dogs but you'll see for yourselves that that's not the case. They're working dogs and they'd be miserable without enough physical activity. Reinar, their owner, takes really good care of them. He's a single man and always will be because he loves his dogs so much that his whole life revolves around them." She laughed. "It's quite an experience. If you think we are isolated, you're in for a surprise when you see where he lives."

"Are we going far?" Kristine asked.

"It's only a forty-minute drive from here," Dani said. "It's not far, but everything takes longer in winter. We'll be sledging along the Russian border. Make sure your phone is fully charged if you want to take pictures, it's really beautiful there."

"I can't wait." Hannah stood up and winked at Kristine when Dani got called away by Sofia and Gunnar, walking over to the buffet to sample the rest of the food. She hadn't expected much from the local cuisine coming here but the few things she'd tasted so far, including last night's soup, were really good and now she was getting awfully curious. Besides the waffles and fresh bread, there were scrambled eggs with fresh dill, smoked salmon and ready-made open sandwiches with a variety of toppings that her fellow diners seemed excited about. She scooped some of the creamy scrambled eggs onto her plate and topped them off with a slice of smoked salmon. As she turned to go back to her table, her eye caught a glimpse of movement outside the window. She walked over and opened the drapes a little further. It was a reindeer, sniffing left-overs that they'd dropped in the snow during last night's dinner. Hannah waved for Kristine to join her.

"What is it?" Kristine asked, lowering her voice as she rushed over.

"Look." Hannah pointed at the window. "It's a reindeer."

Kristine stuck her face through the drapes, her cheek close to Hannah's. "Oh my God, it's a reindeer. Santa's coming," she whispered in Hannah's ear. Hannah shivered at Kristine's breath against her skin. She was standing close behind her, peering out of the window. *Why am I so affected by her?* Although Kristine was gorgeous, Hannah hadn't seen this physical arousal coming.

"What are you guys looking at?" Sarah asked, jerking the drapes completely open. She shrieked when she saw the reindeer. "Josh, come quick!"

The reindeer had spotted the sudden movement behind the window and had taken off, vanishing out of sight.

"Seriously, Josh! You're the one holding the camera and now you've missed it." Sarah sighed, rolling her eyes. "Why do you always have to be so distracted?"

Joshua shifted uncomfortably on his spot, well aware that everyone was looking at him. "I'm sorry, pumpkin," he said.

"She's terrible to him," Kristine whispered in Hannah's ear, still hidden behind the heavy fabric of the drapes. "I feel like I need to stand up for Joshua."

Hannah shrugged. "I think he needs to stand up for himself," she whispered back. "No sympathy whatsoever."

4

## A HUSKY RIDE

Hannah stood on the back of the sled and held on to the handrail while Kristine sat in the small compartment at the front, her legs covered with a blanket. Five Siberian huskies in full harness were hitched to the front of the sled, impatient to start running. This was completely different to what she'd imagined. For starters, there was definitely going to be no snuggling up against Kristine on the small wooden surface, that much was clear. But still, the view was beautiful and she was glad she'd come along. It seemed like madness, being here in the middle of nowhere, in minus four temperatures, and it was the most extreme thing she'd experienced in her life so far. She felt like she'd reached the end of the world. Apart from Reinar's farm, they hadn't seen any sign of human life during the drive here. No lights, no houses, not even a farm. They'd passed a herd of reindeer and had stopped to take pictures, to Sarah's delight, but their flashlights had scared them away. There were some pine trees scattered around but mostly there was just a whole lot of nothing. Endless flats of snow under a clear twilight sky that was a kind of blue she'd never seen in a sky before. It wasn't light blue or aquamarine, like she was used to, but more of a dark cobalt, a saturated dark, a pure blue that was in beautiful contrast to the white stretch that seemed to tip over the edge of the Earth. She shifted her gaze down to Kristine, who looked equally mesmerized by the surreal landscape.

"Ready?" she asked.

"I don't think I've got a choice." Kristine giggled.

"Okay, listen up, people!" Reinar yelled at the group. He raised a hand. "I will ride at the front. The dogs are a tight pack, so they will always follow my alpha's lead. Switch your lights on now, so you don't forget. For the people standing on the back, make sure you move along in the bends, like you would on a bicycle. The metal bar by your feet is the brake. If I lift my hand, it means you need to step on the brake and at the same time, lift your hand so the people behind you know they need to brake too. For the people sitting down in the sled, keep your hands inside, relax and pray that your driver knows what he or she is doing." He laughed. "Halfway, after our lunch break, we'll switch. The driver will sit down in the sled and visa-versa because you'll get tired, even though you think you're not doing very much. Just remember, the dogs love to run and they won't stop if you don't brake. They're like wolves; they can go on for days." He walked along the sleds and checked if anyone had questions. Espen and Dani were both at the back on separate sleds, with the Danish pensioners comfortably in the front. They would ride last to make sure everyone was safe. Reinar stepped onto his own sled and yelled something at his dogs. Hannah held on tight when her dogs suddenly took off, sprinting after Reinar's sled, way faster than she'd anticipated. They picked up speed and before she knew it she was holding on for dear life, her gloved hands firmly gripping the metal bar.

"My God, this is crazy," she shouted.

"Are you okay?" Kristine asked, turning and looking at her.

"Yeah. It's amazing." Hannah bent her left leg, weighing in when the dogs took a turn to avoid a group of trees. "I think I'm getting the hang of it." She was surprised to hear herself laugh out loud. The feeling of speeding through the bare landscape was liberating. Hannah wasn't sure how fast they were going. Maybe the lack of daylight made it seem like they were going much faster than they actually were but she felt a rush each time they reached a bare stretch where the dogs could sprint without having to dodge trees or rocks. She managed to use the brake when Reinar raised his hand, warning them about obstacles, and eventually she started feeling the dogs' movements, anticipating which way they were going without even looking ahead. Kristine was laughing too, looking out from the front compartment as they sped through the wintery landscape.

"This is so much fun!" she yelled, stretching her arms behind her to touch Hannah's hands.

"Yeah? Do you want to go faster?" Hannah's eyes locked with Kristine's when she looked over her shoulder for a moment. Then she let go of the brake entirely and let the dogs run free over a large stretch of crisp, white land.

"RIGHT THERE IS the Russian border crossing," Reinar said during their break, pointing to a long, single-storey building in the far distance with a couple of cars parked in front of it. Bright lights illuminated the land around the border. Hannah glanced over at the building she'd spotted as soon as they'd stopped. She'd been too caught up in the ride to spot it sooner, only vaguely registering the source of light. It looked out of place, as if a man-made building had no business being here. They were seated in the snow, surrounded by the dogs who were delighted with the attention they were getting after the long run. "It's the Storskog border crossing station," Reinar continued. "As you can imagine, it's not the busiest border. My friend Harald works there. He says it's the most boring job in the world but there aren't many other jobs to choose from, unless you work in hospitality."

"Seems like you haven't got it so bad, Reinar. Imagine running a small business here," Sofia added with a frown. "Your customer base would never be more than what, say five to ten people?"

"Out here, certainly." Reinar gave her a lop-sided smile and scratched his beard, removing the icicles that had settled underneath his chin. He looked like a Viking, Hannah thought. Or at least the way she'd always imagined Vikings to look like. Reinar spread his arms. "But living here is a choice. Everyone who lives here actually wants to live here and we're proud of our part of the country. And although the winters can be challenging, dark and lonely, the summers are pleasant, and the days are long. On the first day the snow begins to melt, and people from the countryside, like me, start going into town again, it's a very social affair. The cafés stay open all night sometimes, because the locals are so excited to catch up after months of hibernation. Farmers, fishermen, hotel owners like Espen and Dani... We all flock into town. The people who live in the center of Kirkenes have it easier, though. Tourism is thriving both in winter and summer. The cruise ships stop off there and there's an ice-hotel that people come from all over the world to stay at. Dani told me you are going to have lunch there on

Christmas day." He smiled, playfully fighting with one of his dogs that kept nipping at his heels for attention. "It's a hard life, but it's a good life for people who are suited for it. I wouldn't change it for the world." He took the dog in a tight grip and scratched him roughly over his chest. "I mean, look at these guys. I can't think of any better company to spend my life with."

"How can you tell them apart?" Charlotte asked. "Don't take this the wrong way, we've never had dogs. But they all look the same to me."

"It's easy." Reinar looked lovingly at his pack of dogs. "I raised them. I know their personalities, their likes, their dislikes and their rank in the pack... All thirty of them. I can tell when they're puppies who's going to be the competitive front runner and who will be the one who just likes cuddles and attention and runs along for fun. They're just amazing creatures and companions." Reiner stopped when he realized everyone was looking at him. He cleared his throat with embarrassment and busied himself with the harness of the dog next to him. But his voice cracking with emotion, and the way his face lit up with pride and love for his country and his dogs, had made a lasting impression on his audience. Sofia wiped a tear from her cheek and Gunnar looked emotional too.

Hannah started stroking the two dogs that had decided to lie down next to her, pulling her attention away from Reinar, who clearly regretted making himself the center of attention. They were panting, their eyes wide with excitement from their run.

"I miss my dog now," Kristine said, scratching one of them behind their ears as she sat down next to Hannah on one of the plastic mats they'd brought along.

"You have a dog?" Hannah looked over at her.

"Yeah, Belle. She's a golden retriever. My brother Jed found her wandering along the side of the road when she was a puppy and he gave her to me. He's looking after her while I'm away. She's almost ten now. She's starting to get a bit slow but she still likes her long walks."

"That's so sweet. I'd love to have a dog," Hannah said. "But I could never have one in London with my busy life. I'm at work twelve to fourteen hours a day and dogs aren't allowed in restaurants in the UK."

"I can't imagine a life without a dog now." Kristine kissed the husky she was fussing over on the top of his head. "It's so nice having someone to come home to every day, especially when you live by yourself. She's always happy to see me and I'm always happy to see her." She smiled and nodded towards their sled. "You did a great job there, boss. No accidents. I hope I can offer the same service on our way back."

"I'm sure you'll do fine. You country girls can do anything right? Build things, grow things, fix things...." Hannah took her thermos out of her backpack, filled her cup, took a sip and then offered it to Kristine. "Coffee?"

"I'm not sure about the building and the fixing." Kristine laughed. "But I do grow a lot of vegetables. It's more like a hobby, but I'm proud of my veggie patch and I eat fresh vegetables from it every day." She took the coffee. "Thanks." Although Kristine had her own coffee with her, she liked the idea of sharing with Hannah. There was something intimate about sharing food and drinks with an attractive woman and by now, she couldn't deny that the thought of sharing Hannah's bed had crossed her mind too.

"You grow your own food? That's awesome," Hannah said. "It must be amazing to be able to go into your back garden and pick what you're going to cook for dinner. What do you grow?"

"I've tried just about anything by now." Kristine smiled. "I grow beets, carrots, collards, kale, turnip, garlic, onion and potatoes in winter, and in summer I grow okra, tomatoes, sweet potato, cantaloupe, watermelon, eggplant, pumpkin, peppers and sugar cane, just because those thrive in the climate. I've been trying some Asian vegetables as well in the past years, like edamame and pak choi. It's fun."

"Wow. I wish I could have a garden with my restaurant. It's not always easy to get organic produce all year round. I tried to get permission to build a garden on the roof of my flat but it's been denied three times because it's in a proposed conservation area."

"Do you live far from your restaurant?" Kristine handed the coffee back to Hannah.

"I live above it. It's in Camden, which is a really hip neighborhood in London where all the foodies are congregating right now. We're lucky to be doing really well with so much competition around, but it's a great place to hang out and work during the day, and to eat and celebrate at night. That's probably the reason I never switch off. I spend all of my time there, including my days off. I even have my first coffee there in the morning while I catch up on the news. I like to have a couple of hours to myself before my staff comes in at ten."

"Your life sounds exciting," Kristine said, still fussing over the dog. "I've never even been to London."

"I could say the same thing about you. And I've never been to Covington."

"I think you'd like it... just for a visit," Kristine added. "You'd probably go crazy after two weeks. There's not much to do, apart from visiting New Orleans, which is about an hour from where I live."

"I'm not as wild as you seem to think I am." Hannah

laughed, swiping her dark hair behind her ears and pulling her beanie further over them. "Sure, I go out sometimes, but mostly I just work really hard and watch Netflix in bed before I fall asleep. It's really not that interesting." She settled back on her elbows and grinned. "This, however, is very exciting."

"Yeah. Isn't it something?" Kristine said, looking around the bare, white stretch. "This has surpassed my wildest expectations. Don't you feel weird, just being here? I feel like I'm an intruder." She kept her voice down, as if she were talking to herself. "I'll never, ever understand how life works around here, yet I feel so privileged to be a part of it, even if it's just for five days." She shifted her gaze to Reinar, who was talking to Werner and Charlotte. "Look at him. He's at one with nature. He's chosen to stay here, to live this rough existence. He understands and lives by the rules of the land, and he manages, day in and day out. He's got no one to talk to in winter, apart from his dogs and the tourists he takes on tours, and he'll probably die here all alone. And I can't help but feel this immense respect for him." She paused. "It's like he's got the key to this humble happiness, a secret that we domesticated people have forgotten about."

"I know what you mean." Hannah sighed. "Everything seems so far away and insignificant now. My phone that I'm constantly on, my restaurant, my bookings and deliveries, my staff, my ridiculously expensive coffee maker that I really don't need, those trainers I've been dying to get hold of, and my walk-in wardrobe..." She hesitated. "It really makes you wonder what's really important, doesn't it?" She looked at Kristine, noticing again how beautiful she looked.

Kristine nodded slowly, taking Hannah in too.

"No continental buffet today, I'm afraid," Reinar interrupted them. He handed out lunch boxes from the bag in his sled that Dani had prepared. "But Dani's homemade bread is the best I've ever tasted, that's for sure."

"Thanks," Kristine said. Her hand brushed Hannah's when she took their lunch packs from Reinar and handed one to her, and Hannah saw an instant shift in her when their eyes met for a moment. She knew exactly what Kristine was thinking, she'd felt it too. Just like this morning, the touch of her hand had caused a stir of excitement she couldn't ignore. She blushed as she diverted her gaze, concentrating on her lunch. *My God, this is going to be interesting.*

5

## STEAMY CONVERSATIONS

"I had a really great day." Kristine dipped her cookie in her tea and sat down next to Hannah. Her cheeks were rosy from being outside all day and her hair was done up in a top-knot, static from the cold. Hannah couldn't stop looking at her. She looked beyond cute and every time she opened her mouth to speak, that Southern twang made her even more charming. "Thanks for being my holiday friend." She looked at Hannah, offering her a cookie. "I like spending time with you."

"I like spending time with you too." Hannah took Kristine's hand, brought it to her mouth and took a bite from the cookie. It was an intimate gesture, definitely not something 'holiday friends' who had only just met would do. But she loved how easy everything was with Kristine, how they could talk about anything for hours on end. And then there was the chemistry, which was off the charts. After a ten-year long failed relationship, Hannah had forgotten how it felt to have those butterflies around someone, and she'd imagined more than once what it would be like to kiss her. She was pretty sure Kristine was interested in her too, she was sending out all the right signals. The little touches, her flirtatious comments and the way she looked at her, sometimes longer than necessary...

"So, Christmas Eve tomorrow," Hannah continued, when their eyes locked for so long that she didn't know what else to do but keep the conversation going. She wasn't used to this flutter in her belly. "Anything you'll be wishing for?"

"Northern lights would be great," Kristine said, casting a glance at the sky for a brief moment. "Unfortunately Espen doesn't think it's going to happen tonight either." She raised an eyebrow. "Apart from that..." she opened her mouth to continue, but fell silent, blushing through her already rosy cheeks.

"Apart from that you want what?" Hannah gave her a flirtatious smile. From the look on Kristine's face, she knew exactly where her thoughts were going.

"No... it's nothing, actually. I'm pretty happy." Kristine grinned. "What about you?"

Hannah held her gaze. She wanted to kiss Kristine so badly. That was what she wanted for Christmas. And she didn't just want to kiss her, because once her lips had been on Kristine's she knew that would never be enough. She wanted to rip off all those layers of clothing and have her hands and her mouth all over that amazing body. She wanted to be inside her, pleasure her for hours on end, make her come all night long... But if Kristine wasn't going to say it, she was willing to play the long game too.

"I'm good," she said instead. "Everything is perfect right now. Can't think of anything else I want." She smiled. "Apart from maybe having another twenty minutes in the sauna. And I think I'm going to do that right now."

"Wait!" Kristine looked up at Hannah when she stood up

from her chair. "Do you mind if I join you? I've been dying to try it too but I have no idea how it works."

"Not at all. Come on." Hannah started walking towards the house, so Kristine wouldn't notice her flushed state.

Hannah didn't know where to look when Kristine walked into the small sauna and sat down with only a fluffy, white towel draped around her. She'd wrapped her hair into another towel on top of her head, enhancing her long, elegant neck. Her shoulders were beautiful too; broad and well-defined, and her arms were lean and feminine. But the best part was still her eyes. Kristine's eyes had an intensity to them that was almost too much to handle for Hannah, after their flirtations. Each time she looked into them she got swept away by the light blue hue that made her forget about everything else around her. And now she was in this tiny space with Kristine, both barely covered. She felt a stir of arousal deep down in her core, spreading down to her center, and for the first time in her life, she had no idea what to say.

"Wow, this is way hotter than I expected, Kristine said," finally breaking the silence. She looked Hannah up and down with a playful smile on her lips. "Way, way hotter than I ever imagined." She failed to rid herself of the mischievous smile as she pointed towards the hot stones, piled up in a sealed compartment. "Want to show me how it works?"

"Sure. It's really simple, actually." Hannah fought to keep a straight face, pretending she hadn't heard the sexual undertone in Kristine's comment, simply because she had no idea how to reply to it. She picked up the bucket of water by the door, grateful for some distraction from her impure thoughts. "Basically, you just slowly add water if you want to up the humidity. Higher humidity makes it more tolerable." She poured some water over the stones, causing steam to rise up to the ceiling and spread out towards the four corners of the sauna before it started to drop down slowly.

"That easy, huh? I could have done that myself yesterday." Kristine sighed. "And *now* what do we do?"

Hannah could tell Kristine was starting to get slightly uncomfortable with the heat, wincing and taking quick breaths.

"Now, we sit back and relax. Are you okay? Is it too hot for you? I can open the door for a bit if you're uncomfortable." Hannah stood up and pushed open the door for a couple of seconds.

"Thank you, I can breathe now." Kristine rolled her eyes. "I'm sorry, I should leave. I'm ruining your sauna experience with my whining about it being too hot. That's the whole point, isn't it?"

"No, please stay." Hannah begged. "You're not ruining it at all. It's nice to have you here." She took a deep breath, enjoying the hot steam that made her sweat from every single pore in her body while she marveled over how great Kristine looked without her clothes on. "Have a cold shower after this and scrub," she said in a soft voice. "It'll remove all your dead skin cells and you'll be silky smooth in the morning. It relaxes your muscles too, so you won't have as much muscle ache from walking in the snow today and, on top of that, it flushes out toxins and makes you sleep like a baby."

"I don't think I'll have any trouble with the sleeping part," Kristine joked. "So, how come you know so much about saunas?"

Hannah shrugged. "I don't, really. Hasn't everyone been in a sauna once or twice in their lives?"

"Not where I come from." Kristine shifted on the bench opposite Hannah, making her towel creep a little further up her thighs. Hannah tried her hardest not to look. This was definitely a welcome change from sitting opposite Werner.

"Of course, I forgot," she said, a little flushed when she couldn't help but look down at Kristine's thighs anyway. "You don't need a sauna; you can just go outside in summer, right?"

"Yeah, I suppose so. Louisiana can be really warm in summer. Sometimes to the point where it's unbearable." She paused. "But I do like the summers. We have picnics and barbecues and we paddle down the bayou or just relax by the water on weekends. Sometimes I rent a stall at one of the local farmers markets to sell vegetables when I have too much to give away. Just for fun."

"That sounds really nice." Hannah opened the door for another couple of seconds to give Kristine a bit more air.

"It is." Kristine smiled. "I complain a lot about the boring, sleepy village I live in, and sometimes I panic, because I think I'll never get out of there. But every time I'm away, or when I talk to someone about Covington on my travels, I feel this renewed appreciation, and I start longing to be home again. I guess sometimes we don't realize what's right under our nose, huh?"

"Don't we all make that mistake? Hannah asked. "I complain about how hectic my life is all the time. And in theory, it sounds like a dream to me, to be able to have picnics on weekends, or to take a boat out and have fun with friends. But when it comes down to it, I love London, and I love my restaurant. It would take a lot for me to give it up. I get a kick out of busy nights, when I'm fully booked and collapse after 2am. That's when I realize I've done something right, that I've fought for what I wanted and succeeded, and I wouldn't want to trade it for the world."

"We should count ourselves pretty lucky then." Kristine's

eyes shifted to Hannah's cleavage and Hannah realized her towel had dropped a little, revealing a nipple. She lifted her towel back up and tightened it under her armpit, folding the loose edge into the fabric draped around her. "I'm sorry, I should have said something, but I..." Kristine fell silent, her eyes darkening.

"It's fine," Hannah reassured her. "You've seen boobs before, right? Nothing new there."

Kristine shook her head with an uncomfortable giggle. "I certainly have." She laughed again and stood up. "Is it hot in here? It's really hot, isn't it?"

"Yeah, it's hot. It's a sauna." Hannah paused and quirked an eyebrow at Kristine. "Or was it my beautiful, perky, perfect nipple that made your temperature rise?" Her tone was teasing. The fact that Kristine was thrown off her game made her confidence rise and she was having fun with it now.

"Maybe. It's been a while since I've seen one." Kristine opened the door. "Well, thank you for the show. I'm going to have that cold shower that you recommended." She gave Hannah a quick wave, avoiding eye-contact, then slipped out of the sauna.

Hannah dropped her towel on the floor and fell down onto the bed, lacking the energy to take a shower, even though she was still boiling after the sauna. She was familiar with jetlag but the constant dark was a whole new level of confusion. The twilight that settled during the afternoon made her subconsciously wait for the sun to come up, yet it never happened. She glanced at her phone that had no signal. The two messages from her head chef, that had come in a couple of hours ago, were still unread, but the words 'fantastic', 'busy' and 'great' told her all she needed to know, so she was in no rush to attempt a reply. It would only waste hours, so he was prepared for her lack of communication. She was amused when she saw that it was only 10pm. Hannah never went to bed before 2am, normally. Closing up a restaurant was a time-consuming task. Dividing the tips, counting the till while her staff were having drinks at the bar, chatting and laughing, some of the younger waitresses planning on where they'd be going next. Then there was inventory, emergency orders and leftovers that had to be used up the next day during lunch, which meant tweaking the menu... Hannah was usually at her best late at night but now, she could barely keep her eyes open. It felt like midnight, but despite her tiredness, she kind of liked how day and night were one and the same here. How there was no time, nothing to hang on to. It had been an interesting evening, one that left her wanting more. Kristine had been flirtatious. Hannah had been flirtatious too. Hell, she'd seen her nipple tonight and, although that didn't seem like such a big deal, Kristine had left in a hurry with a bright blush on her cheeks. There was obvious sexual tension between them and it had only grown stronger as the days had passed.

Kristine had been joking over breakfast when she'd told Hannah that the lack of light was making her giddy but, somehow, Hannah knew she'd meant what she'd said. There was something about the dark that made people speak their minds and that made people bond. Hannah had warmed to everyone in the group today, even to Sarah a little. The dark was making her think much more and much deeper than she normally would. It was also making her unusually honest, apparently. Even after only two days here, she'd started to open up and have deep conversations with people she would never talk to in such a way back home. Not because she didn't want to but simply because she never felt the need to open up. In her daily life, Hannah was a people person, a pleaser. It came naturally to her and that worked wonders with her clientele. She knew how to bind people to her and customers always came back, often weekly. But the contact was always superficial and never went further than a few jokes or inquiring about their business or their family. Here, she'd had deep conversations with Kristine, and even the unexpected sauna encounter with Werner that morning had turned out to be quite frankly fascinating, with his stories about being stationed in Ethiopia and Angola during the wars there and about living in East Germany before the wall came down. It was the strangest thing. She wondered whether she would change deeply if she were to spend more time here. *What if ...* Hannah blinked a couple of times before her eyes fell shut, her thoughts lulling her into slumber while she still lay on top of the covers.

## 6

# MEMORIES

Hannah snoozed three times before she managed to open her eyes. The lack of light still made it feel unnatural to even consider getting out of bed, but it was getting a little easier now, on the third day. The high-tech light system installed in her room mimicked the pattern of a faint sunrise each morning, just enough to be able to see without the nightstand lamp on. It was subtle, and she hadn't even realized until now that the occasional birdsong she heard was coming from the speakers in her room, and not from outside her window. Any more light would have brought her body into confusion when she got outside, as it was pitch dark, and any less would have left her asleep. Now, she was in that vague state in between but that was good enough to stomach a coffee and some breakfast. Next to her bed was a figurine of what she now knew to be a 'nisse' - a short old man with a beard and a knitted cap. He was carved out of wood, but the cap was made out of real wool, and his beard consisted of something that looked uncomfortably close to real hair. He resembled a friendly garden gnome. The mythical Norwegian mischievous creatures only came out over Christmas, apparently.

"Hey, little dude," she mumbled as she turned over to face him. She felt excited about the day ahead and she was pretty sure the presence of a certain attractive blonde had something to do with that. Although Hannah's worst pain after Beth's departure had subsided, mornings were still hard, and the decision to get away from the apartment that they used to share over Christmas had been a wise one.

She remembered it like it was yesterday, waking up alone, wondering why Beth was up so early on a Monday morning. Monday was their day off and they usually stayed in bed until at least midday, catching up on sleep after a hard week's work. She'd gone down to check the restaurant in case Beth was making herself a coffee but there had been no sign of her. It wasn't until she got back to their bedroom that she'd spotted the pink Post-it Note on her nightstand table. They always left each other notes when the other was still sleeping, the messages usually ending with three kisses or a heart. There were no kisses that day, just a short message. Hannah had still been smiling when she'd picked up the note, expecting to find a sweet message, something like 'just gone out to get us some breakfast' or 'couldn't sleep, went for a run, love u'. She remembered the cold that spread inside her as she'd re-read the note, unable to understand Beth's message initially.

*I'm sorry Hannah. I love you, but I can't do this anymore. I feel like I'm suffocating, and I need to get away. You can have it all. Please take care of Ziggy.*

Her handwriting had been messy, and some letters had been scribbled out, as if she'd written it in a rush. It was the last Post-it Note Beth would ever leave her. Hannah then ran into their dressing room to check if Beth's things were gone.

Most of her clothes were still there, but her favorite pieces were missing and so was her leather duffel bag. By that point, she'd almost choked in shock as the realization hit her that it wasn't a dream or a joke. She'd sprinted downstairs to check the top drawer of the bureau in the living room, only to find that Beth's passport and bank cards were gone too. That had been the moment Hannah's world had collapsed. It had taken her months to accept that Beth wasn't coming back and, as time had passed, anger had taken over from the pain. She'd only recently heard from mutual friends that Beth had gone traveling and was currently working at a beach bar in some hippie resort in Thailand. For Hannah, knowing that she hadn't been enough to make Beth happy had been the hardest thing to accept. That and not knowing how long Beth had been unhappy, how long she'd been thinking of escaping their life together. She acknowledged that she was partly to blame, as she'd apparently missed the signs that Beth was miserable. She'd been so preoccupied with her restaurant, that she'd selfishly never given any thought to Beth's wishes, assuming her dream was Beth's dream too. But it hadn't been Beth's dream. She'd studied archaeology, which was her passion. A lack of interesting vacancies in the field, and a natural talent for organization and finance, had led her to work alongside Hannah for apparently longer than she could bear. They had a restaurant together, an apartment, a car, a cat... Technically, Ziggy - their tabby - was Beth's cat. She'd brought her along when she'd moved in with Hannah, who was just in the process of starting her restaurant back then. Ziggy never slept in the bed after Beth was gone, and she never cuddled up on Hannah's lap like she used to, as if she blamed Hannah for chasing Beth away. She was out most of the day and only came in to eat, or to sleep on the top bookshelf. Hannah had tried so hard to get into Ziggy's good books. She'd even brought her fresh chicken thighs from her kitchen each day, but after six months, Ziggy was still reluctant to bond, peering at Hannah with suspicion in her sharp eyes each time she approached her.

Beth had gotten more involved with the restaurant over the years and, in the last two years they were together, she'd taken care of all the finances, the bookings and their staff. She'd been just as invested in the restaurant as Hannah was – or so Hannah thought - and she'd never complained, never let a word slip about not being happy, about not liking her job or the responsibilities she'd taken on. She'd simply left one day, just like that. Hannah had stalked her on social media for a while but seeing Beth with a big smile on some exotic beach in most of the pictures only fuelled her anger, and she'd finally let it go, realising she was starting to turn into a bitter mess. It was then that she'd started sleeping around, trying to move on. She'd be out looking for women on her nights off, avoiding her empty apartment that always reminded her of what she'd lost.

It had been just over six months now, but mornings were still hard each time she woke up and turned towards her nightstand. The pile of Post-it Notes was gone and so was the vase that used to hold the flowers Beth bought at their local market each Friday. Being away from that nightstand for a short week had been good for Hannah and she realized she hadn't even thought of Beth since the day she'd arrived, apart from the brief conversation with Kristine when she'd mentioned her. Just like the many one-night stands she'd had before she came here, her flirtations with Kristine were a welcome distraction from the emptiness Beth had left when she'd disappeared from her life. Beth's sudden departure had seriously bruised her ego too and sleeping around had been Hannah's form of therapy. The kind that had patched her back together and made her feel better about herself again, even if it was just for a little while. The big difference here was that she couldn't escape Kristine the next morning. She was getting to know her and she genuinely liked her. Not only did Hannah like Kristine, she was getting more intrigued by her as the days passed and she couldn't seem to stop thinking about her. She liked being near Kristine. Their flirting was getting to the point where it couldn't pass as a joke anymore. It was serious, full-on flirting. But there was no harm in that, right? They were only here for three more nights and, so far, nothing had happened. *Not yet.* Hannah knew she wanted to change that and she could tell by the way Kristine looked at her, that she might want that too.

## 7

## A BAKING LESSON

"What the hell are you wearing, Josh?" Sarah asked from behind her coffee cup. Josh looked down at his outfit, puzzled as to what was wrong with it.

"What do you mean pumpkin? I thought this was what you wanted me to wear?"

"Not the green one." Sarah rolled her eyes like she always did whenever Joshua opened his mouth to speak. "The blue sweater, Josh. The green one's for Christmas Day, I told you that." Hannah and Kristine exchanged amused glances, while taking in Josh's outfit which looked perfectly acceptable.

"Okay..." Josh shrugged. "I'll go and change then."

"Never mind. It's too late, everyone's seen your Christmas sweater now. You might as well keep it on." Josh lingered by the table until Sarah patted the chair next to her. "Come on, let's eat. Want me to make you something?"

"Someone please shoot me if I ever become like her," Kristine whispered. "I bet she won't even let him tie his own shoelaces."

Hannah shrugged. "He seems quite happy in his role. He doesn't look like he minds being bossed around to be honest. The way he looks at her..." They both glanced over at Josh who was staring at Sarah lovingly while she made him a sandwich.

"Yeah, you might be right." Kristine furrowed her brow and shook her head. "Still, it seems wrong. People should be equal in relationships. I dated this woman once who insisted on opening every door for me, paying for everything and planning every little detail of our dates. She even bought me dresses to wear before we went on a date... She meant well but after a couple of weeks I'd had enough. I literally wanted to strangle her."

"Well, let's hope nobody gets killed over the next couple of days then." Hannah shot Kristine a teasing look. "Want me to make you a sandwich, pumpkin?" At that, they both burst out in hysterical laughter, attracting attention from their fellow guests.

"It's nothing," Kristine said, waving a hand at the others, huddled around the breakfast buffet. "Hannah's just being silly." She nudged Hannah's leg with her foot under the table and Hannah took the opportunity to clamp it between her calves. She had no idea why she'd done it but Kristine didn't seem to mind and relaxed back into her chair, her foot comfortably resting in between Hannah's legs. They stared at each other for a couple of seconds, both enjoying the physical contact. Kristine shot Hannah a flirty smile and lowered her voice. "Maybe I'll let you make me that sandwich after all."

"ARE you sure you want to spend the day in the kitchen, Hannah?" Kristine joked when Hannah returned from her room after breakfast, still only wearing leggings and a hoodie. Espen was taking some of the hotel guests ice-fishing and for those who didn't want to go; Dani had organized a baking session in preparation for Christmas.

Hannah grinned sheepishly. "Yes, well you know how I said I didn't want anything to do with food on my holiday? I can't seem to help myself. I'm curious about these cookies and I don't want to miss the chance to learn how to bake them." She didn't mention that the main reason she was there was to spend as much time with Kristine as possible.

"To be honest, I didn't expect anything different from you." Kristine laughed. "I'm not much of a baker myself but it's too early in the morning for me to watch Espen gut a fish, so I'm quite comfortable here. I'm a bit of a hypocrite like that. I'll happily eat a fish but I'll most likely cry if I see one get caught and killed."

"Me too," Sofia chipped in, joining them in front of the fireplace. "But Gunnar couldn't believe his luck. Fishing is his all-time favorite hobby." She rolled her eyes. "He was mentally preparing himself in our room this morning. He's got a competitive streak, so God forbid someone catches a bigger fish than him."

"So, you guys want to help me bake?" Dani handed Kristine, Hannah and Sofia an apron each, beckoning them to come into the kitchen. It was a lot more spacious than Hannah had expected, with professional appliances and two big, industrial ovens.

"Nice kitchen," she remarked.

"Thanks." Dani smiled proudly. "We had it renovated last year. It was quite challenging to cook for big groups in our old kitchen. Now it's a delight." She walked over to the cooking island in the middle of the kitchen, already laid out with all the ingredients. “I believe you used to be a chef?” she said to Hannah.

“Used to be, yeah. Sadly I don’t spend much time in the kitchen anymore; I’m mainly front of house now. But I do love to bake.” Hannah rubbed her hands together. “I’m excited to learn all about your Christmas cookies.”

“Great.” Dani put on her own apron and turned to her students for the day. “Let me tell you first that here in Norway, baked goods are really important all year around. If it’s your birthday, you have to bake at least one cake for your guests but most people bake two or three. With Christmas, it’s a tradition to make a selection of seven different kinds of cookies to eat at home and to give out to family and friends.”

“Seven? God, that sounds time consuming,” Sofia said.

“It is. But now I’ve got your help, you can all make one type each.” She winked at Hannah. “Or you could make two varieties and then I’ll only have to make three.”

Hannah laughed. “No pressure. Bring it on.”

“There’s nothing complicated or technical about them, it’s all about the spice mix. I’ll show you what to do, and you’ll have the recipes, so don’t worry.” Dani handed out the recipes and gave them each their own space on the island. “I bought a stock of butter last month, because we always have a shortage in town this time of the year when everyone bakes enough for a small army.”

Kristine was making ‘berlinerkranser’, prepared with cooked egg yolks and raw egg yolks. Sofia’s duty was making ‘sandkaker’, with a base of ground almonds, and Hannah was tasked with making ‘sirupsnippers’, using cinnamon, star anise, pepper and ginger as the main spices, and also with making little doughnut shaped sugary treats, called ‘smultringer’. Dani was making ‘goro’, which were vanilla flavored waffle cookies, baked in a rectangular hot patterned iron, 'krumkake', crispy wafer-like cookies baked in a large round iron and then rolled around a cone-shaped cake stick, and 'fattigman', which translated into 'poor man's cakes', deep fried diamond shaped cookies with brandy in them and bejeweled in powdered sugar.

"I usually have a couple of shots while I'm baking these but this year, I'll have to pass on the tradition," Dani said, patting her belly.

"Are you pregnant?" Hannah asked.

Dani beamed. "Thirteen weeks now. It's only just starting to feel real. We told Espen's parents last week, before you came, and we called my father in Oslo."

"Congratulations, that's wonderful," Kristine said, giving her a hug. Hannah and Sofia hugged her too.

"Thank you. We're very happy." She smiled and filled three shot glasses with brandy, filling one for herself with orange juice before handing them out to the women. "I haven't even told my friends yet, it feels strange to say it out loud."

"Let's toast to the baby then." Hannah held up her shot glass.

"Really? Brandy at ten in the morning?" Sofia laughed but downed the brandy anyway. "Cheers to your baby, Dani."

"It's not uncommon here in winter to have an early shot." Dani winked. "It's cold so a lot of people have an akevitt - or aquavit, as you English say it - with their coffee in the morning. It's distilled from grains and potatoes and flavored with herbs. It warms you up before you go outside. We've arranged an akevitt tasting for tomorrow afternoon, so you'll be able to sample some local spirits."

"That sounds fun. I'd better pace myself today then," Kristine said, declining a second shot of brandy. She watched Hannah roll up her sleeves and get stuck in, mixing her ingredients. It was sexy, the way she was working the dough like a pro, and she looked strong and capable despite her slim frame. Kristine forced herself to concentrate on her recipe instead of on Hannah's arms. She found it a lot harder than the three other women made it look. Even Sofia seemed to know exactly what she was doing, mixing fast and tasting the raw dough, adding more spices or sugar when she judged necessary. Her own hands were covered in the sticky dough, blobs of the mixture reaching all the way up to her left elbow.

"Here, let me help you with that." Hannah laughed as she peeled the dough off Kristine's hands and wrists. "Use a little more flour; it will make it less sticky." She dusted the workbench in front of them with flour, gathered the dough and started kneading it with one hand. "Use your wrist, like this." Then she took Kristine's hand, put it on top of the dough and covered it with her own hand, guiding her.

Kristine held her breath at the closeness, cursing the blush she felt creeping up her neck towards her face. Hannah was standing slightly behind her now, her mouth close to her ear. She could feel her heart thumping in her throat and couldn't help but wonder how the hell baking could be so erotic.

"That's good," Hannah said. "You've got it. Now shape it into a ball and put it back in the bowl, it needs to rest in the fridge."

"Thank you." Kristine didn't dare look up as she shaped her dough with trembling hands, scared that Hannah would see the naked desire in her eyes.

"Are you from Oslo then?" Sofia asked Dani. "You mentioned your father lives there." She was pressing her dough into small round tins with waffle shaped sides.

"Yes. Oslo is my home town. Have you been there?" Dani asked.

"Oh, yes. Gunnar and I have visited there a couple of times. We love the city." Sofia frowned, studying Dani. "Don't you miss it? How do you do it? I mean, living out here, in the middle of nowhere."

Dani smiled. "I was just like you and Hannah, a city girl. Came here on holiday. Although I'm Norwegian, I'd never seen the northern lights before. When I saw Espen's hotel advertised on a website, I was strangely drawn to it. I was working for a travel agent at the time and I wanted to go and check it out. It was only a weekend visit with one of my best friends." She sighed and looked up at her fellow bakers, still mixing her batter. "And the moment I saw Espen, I knew he was the one I wanted to spend the rest of my life with. That rugged look and his naughty schoolboy grin... He was running the hotel with his brother Lasse back then. Lasse moved to Denmark three months later, when he married a Danish woman. It was December when I came here for the first time, not quite Christmas though. And I remember wondering how anyone could live out here. Long-term, I mean." She stopped whisking and slammed the whisk on the edge of the stainless-steel sink. "Espen and I got talking on the first night. We talked for hours, and my friend got annoyed with me because I only had eyes for him, but I couldn't help myself." She smiled. "And now, three years later, we're married and having a baby together."

"That's such a romantic story." Hannah sighed. "Didn't you find it hard though, moving here? I mean, you lived in Oslo, and I've never been there, but I imagine it's the polar opposite of Kirkenes."

"Of course it was hard, at first." Dani added the first batch of batter to her waffle iron and closed it, scraping off the excess batter that was seeping through the sides with a wooden ladle. "I travelled here a couple of weekends a month when we first started dating but it was a long drive. Espen couldn't come to Oslo because of the hotel, so it was always me traveling. After six months of deliberation and endless conversations, Espen asked me if I was interested in replacing Lasse when he left." She rolled her eyes. "I guess it was his way of being romantic and asking me if I wanted to move in with him. So, I decided to take the leap and go for it. I couldn't really imagine my life without him, so staying in Oslo wasn't an option either. I resigned from my job, left my old life behind and started over. By then, I knew exactly what I was getting myself into but nothing could have prepared me for the effect that the changing seasons here would have on my body and mind. I couldn't sleep during the summer and I was tired all the time in winter. Sometimes, I never even woke up when I had a day off. But then another summer came, and then another winter, and it got easier because I knew what to expect. And now, after three years, I'm totally settled and happy, and I can't imagine myself living anywhere else in the world." She turned to Hannah and shot a fleeting glance at Kristine. "There's something magical here, something that makes it easy to fall in love. The precious hours of twilight, the stars, the aurora... You haven't seen it yet but I'm almost certain you will, and when you've experienced it you'll know what I mean. The sheer wonder of it makes people open up, makes them more vulnerable. The summers are magical too. It's strange at first that the sun never goes down but you overcome insomnia eventually and start to appreciate the light when you know you're going to be missing it for months to come in winter."

"Midnight sun," Kristine said. "I've read about it and it's

another thing to experience on my bucket list." She sighed wishfully. "I think I might have to come back in six months' time."

"We call it Sankthansaften here," Dani said. "When I lived in Oslo, I always celebrated it, each year on the twenty-third of June, but never in a place where the sun stays up for twenty-four hours. You can read a newspaper outside at 3am. It's not the same as normal daylight, though. It's like this mystical orange glow, almost red. We have bonfires on the beach and dance all night. They say that if a girl puts flowers under her pillow on midsummer's eve, she will dream of her future husband. Or wife I suppose, in your case." She looked up at Hannah and Kristine again.

"Can you tell?" Kristine asked, staring at her curiously. People were always surprised when she told them she was gay because she didn't fit any of the stereotypes about gay women, which were unfortunately still widespread. Her long blonde hair, her tan and her feminine way of moving often confused people when she told them she was a lesbian. So far, it had been more of a curse than a blessing. On one occasion, during a first date, she'd even been accused by the woman of using her to fulfil some bi-curious fantasy.

"Not by your appearance." Dani laughed. "It's your energy. I'm sensitive so I pick up on it. People give off a certain energy and it tells you a lot about them if you pay attention. So yes, I could tell straight away that you're both into women." She turned back to her waffle-iron. "Not that it makes any difference to me; I was just including you into the story. We have a lot of myths here in Norway but none of them include two women living happily ever after, even though we're very liberal and most of the girls in this country have experimented at some point." She winked and shot them a grin.

"Are you two both..." Sofia's eyes widened as she stared at Hannah and Kristine. "I've never really met a lesbian before. And now I'm in the presence of two!"

Hannah laughed. "If you live in Copenhagen, I'm sure you've come across lesbians at some point. You probably just haven't realized it."

"Yeah, it can be hard to tell sometimes. We're just like real people," Kristine chipped in, teasing Sofia.

"I'm sorry, I didn't mean it that way, I..." Sofia's cheeks turned red.

"Hey, don't worry about it, we're only joking," Kristine interrupted her, rubbing Sofia's shoulder to reassure her.

Dani chuckled at their conversation as she removed the paper-thin waffle from the iron, then skillfully rolled it around the dough stick while it was still warm. When she pulled off the perfect cone-shaped cookie, Hannah clapped.

"Bravo. I can tell you've done that before." She took the cookie from Dani and inhaled the scent of vanilla. "Can I try it?"

"Go ahead." Dani turned back to her iron and poured another ladle of batter over the cast iron surface before closing it.

Hannah bit into the cookie, then passed it to Sofia and Kristine to have a taste. "Mmm... really good," she mumbled through a mouthful. "So light... so yummy. I love the texture and the hint of vanilla."

Dani grinned. "I'm delighted to have your approval, chef."

"Don't call me chef just yet," Hannah joked. "Let's see how these bad boys turn out first." She turned back to her workspace and started cutting out the shapes for her syrupsnippers, placing an almond in the middle of each cookie.

"LOOK WHAT WE'VE GOT HERE!" Gunnar carried an enormous trout into the kitchen, interrupting their conversation as Hannah, Kristine, Sofia and Dani were talking over coffee around the cooking island, waiting for the last batch of cookies to bake.

"Well done! There's dinner for tonight." Dani clapped her hands.

"My God, that's a big one," Hannah said, taking a step aside so he could drop the heavy fish onto the island.

"Did you get a picture with it?" Sofia asked, rubbing her hands over Gunnar's cold, red cheeks.

"Sure did." He was grinning from ear to ear as he took off his hat and his gloves. "It's one of the biggest ones I've ever caught."

Sofia helped him remove his coat, then turned to Dani. "Do you want me to clean the fish for you? I don't want you to get nauseated, now that you're pregnant. I remember when I was pregnant for the first time. I couldn't stand being around raw fish."

"That would be wonderful, actually. Thank you." Dani cast Sofia a grateful smile as she glanced down at the fish, its neck cut from one gill to the other. "I haven't had bad morning sickness so far but there are certain things I struggle with, and that's definitely one of them."

"Bakers!" Espen joined them in the kitchen with another smaller trout in his hands. "Gunnar was hands-down the star today." He lifted the fish he was holding. "Shall I throw this one in the freezer, Dani? We can have it next week when my parents are over." He bagged the fish and took it into the pantry, swiftly returning. "I'm going to get us a Christmas tree now. It's about time. Anyone want to join me?"

Hannah held up a hand. "I'd love to."

"Me too," Kristine said with a big smile.

"Great." He took off his gloves and warmed his hands over the waffle iron that was still hot. "If you two get dressed, I'll get the sled from the garage. It'll be too heavy to carry home."

Hannah and Kristine followed Espen into the woods, all three manned with a flashlight. Espen was carrying his rifle and a bunch of rope around his neck, Hannah an axe, and Kristine was pulling the sled behind her. It was a tough hike, with snow reaching up to their knees in some places. Kristine didn't mention she was terrified each time she heard something rustling, and she made sure to stay close behind Espen and Hannah, clamping onto her flashlight for dear life. She was relieved when they finally reached the spruces, so they wouldn't have to venture further into the woods. They were beautiful trees, some as tall as a house, all covered in a thick layer of snow.

"Take your pick," Espen said. "I have a license to take down seven trees in the month of December. Five are in the bedrooms and one is on the porch, so choose wisely." He laughed as he produced a measuring tape from his pocket. "Just in case. We don't want it to be too high for the living room." Hannah and Kristine walked around, trying to find a suitable spruce.

"This is fun," Kristine said, inspecting the trees. "I've always bought my Christmas trees in town, so this is a really unique experience. Please stay close to me, though. I didn't want to say it, but I'm actually a little scared. It's so dark here."

Hannah glanced over her shoulder at Espen, who was

distracted with the rope, preparing the sled. She took Kristine's hand and pulled her closer, feeling her heart thump in her throat.

"I just have a fake tree in the restaurant," she said casually, pretending not to be affected by Kristine, so close to her now. "I don't even bother in my flat."

"You don't have a real tree?" Kristine whispered. She looked down at their hands, then back up, meeting Hannah's gaze. "How can you not have a real tree at Christmas?"

Hannah shrugged, all too aware of the contact and the fact that Kristine was enjoying it just as much as she was. "I never really cared about Christmas. But... I think I'm slowly changing my mind, building good memories, instead of bad ones."

"Bad?" Kristine looked at her. "What do you mean?"

Hannah shrugged. "Let's just say Christmas was never really a time of celebration when I was younger. But that was a long time ago and I don't want to talk about that." She searched for Kristine's eyes and tightened the grip on her hand. "I'm too happy right now."

"Okay," Kristine gave her a small smile. "I'm really happy too." Her eyes dropped to Hannah's lips and for a moment, she thought of leaning in and kissing her.

"Have you found one yet, ladies?" Espen yelled. Kristine let go of Hannah's hand before the light of his torch could reach them.

"Eh... yeah, I think so," she yelled back, frantically looking around for a reasonably short spruce.

"There's one right here'" Hannah said, shaking the snow off the branches of a perfectly shaped medium sized spruce.

"Good choice," Espen said. "Mind if I take a picture of

the two of you in front of the tree for our website?" He took his phone out of his pocket.

"Sure." Hannah blinked a couple of times, almost blinded by the bright light from his flashlight. She put an arm around Kristine's waist and pulled her in. They both smiled while Espen took a couple of pictures. Then he pointed at the axe Hannah was still holding in her hand. "Will you do the honors?"

8

## CHRISTMAS EVE

"Merry Christmas," Espen shouted from the head of the table, holding up a glass of red wine. "I know most of you, apart from Sofia and Gunnar, don't celebrate until Christmas Day but in Norway, Christmas starts on Christmas Eve." The tables in the cozy dining room had been pulled together and covered with red table cloths, candles, and silver and gold Christmas crackers. Everyone was now gathered around the feast that Dani had spent all afternoon preparing, the centerpiece consisting of the enormous fresh trout that Gunnar had caught, steamed with butter and dill and displayed on a large tray with potato salad, beetroot and pickled cucumber. Gunnar had taken a seat right in front of it, beaming with pride. There was also roast pork belly, sauerkraut, mashed swede, creamed potatoes, homemade gravy and lingonberry jam. Christmas music was softly playing in the background, heightening the festive atmosphere. The tree that Hannah had chopped down from the forest had been decorated after they'd returned. It was next to the table, its pine fumes mixing with the delicious aromas from the food. The tree reached all the way up to the ceiling, full and fresh, hung with gold tinsel and adorned with hand-carved wooden angels painted in red, white and gold. On the top was a crystal angel with a light inside, spreading a dreamy pattern of light specks across the walls and the ceiling.

"Christmas Eve is very important here," Espen continued. "It's the one night that the whole family comes together." He winked at Dani with a big grin. "And soon, we will have a family of our own because Dani is thirteen weeks pregnant." Dani smiled broadly, patting her belly as she joined him at the head of the table. That brought cheering from the group, although word had spread fast and most people were already aware of her pregnancy following their baking session earlier. Congratulations were flying around and people stood up to give Dani a hug. Espen held up his hand, indicating he wasn't done talking yet. Hannah could tell he was already tipsy from the wine. His eyes were glazed and his cheeks ruddy but he seemed very happy.

"But tonight," he continued, "you are our family and this will be the last Christmas that Dani will let me get drunk, so I sincerely hope you don't mind me having a bottle or two." He laughed along with everyone else. "Now, let's raise a glass and say Merry Christmas in Norwegian. God Jul!"

"God Jul!" Everyone yelled back in unison. Hannah felt all warm and fuzzy inside at the sound of clinking glasses and laughter around her. She and her fellow guests had gotten to know each other better and, by now, everyone looked as comfortable as they would be in their own home. She'd never thought she would spend Christmas with a bunch of strangers but it was her best Christmas so far, she decided. Normally she'd be at work now, playing the hostess, troubleshooting, then falling into bed, too exhausted to celebrate Christmas in any way. Not that she cared much for it, she'd never felt that famous spirit that everyone around her obsessed about, but tonight there was definitely a sparkle. She stood up and cheered with everyone, before finally clinking her glass with Kristine's, who was sitting next to her.

"Merry Christmas," she said, and smiled.

"Merry Christmas to you too." Kristine looked at her while she took a sip from her wine. "I think coming here might have been the best idea I've ever had."

"I think I'll agree with that," Hannah said. She held her gaze and felt her stomach flutter. There was an unspoken understanding between them, a strange kind of magic in the air. She couldn't ignore the pull any longer. "Here's to tonight."

A flirty smile was playing around Kristine's mouth. She had stopped trying to hide her desire. They both seemed to be on the same wavelength and all she could think of now was kissing Hannah's delicious mouth.

"Fish?" Werner said.

"Oh... thank you." Kristine woke up from her fantasy and took the heavy tray from him, holding it out for Hannah to help herself before they swapped.

Dinner was loud, fun and festive. They feasted on the food, drank wine, pulled Christmas crackers and laughed about the jokes in them, wearing the golden paper crowns as they socialized. Charlotte, who had been the quiet one in the group up until now, was really coming out of her shell, chatting away about her children and her students, who she almost seemed to love equally. Sarah was yapping at Josh throughout dinner, reminding him to eat his vegetables and to use his napkin, and Sofia and Gunnar seemed pretty tipsy from the red wine already, sharing dirty Danish jokes with Espen and Dani, the punchlines making them cry with laughter. Hannah felt a happiness she couldn't quite comprehend. They really were a family tonight and Kristine, next to her, was giving off all the right signals for an even more exciting night ahead.

Dani suddenly stood up from the table and walked towards the window. "Finally!" she said, turning back to her guests. "Aurora is coming, I can feel it. Get dressed and get out there. Espen will start the fire and I'll bring the dessert outside."

"Do you need help?" Kristine asked her when everyone rushed upstairs to put on their snow gear.

"Yeah. We'll help you clear the table," Hannah said.

"No, just go." Dani laughed. "I've seen it hundreds of times, and it will last for a while, so don't worry. Thank you though. You've both been great helping me out."

IT TOOK a while for anything to happen and Kristine was trying not to get her hopes up too much. They were sitting around the fire again, eating cinnamon rice porridge and drinking coffee and mulled wine.

"Be patient," Espen said. "It will come. Dani is never wrong. She's only been here for three years but she's very intuitive and I trust her predictions way more than I trust my own." He poured himself more mulled wine and passed the thermos to Werner next to him. "Aurora borealis, what you're about to see, or rather experience, originates from the surface of the sun and it travels all the way here to create a spectacle in the sky. It's caused by solar wind, electronically charged solar particles that have been thrown into space. When they reach the Earth's atmosphere and collide with its particles, the explosion can be seen from here up to three or four days later. Dani thinks it's magic, rather than science. I'd say decide for yourself. One myth claims that aurora are torches held in the hands of spirits seeking the souls of people who have recently passed. In some countries the appearance of the aurora was seen to be a bad omen. It is said that the skies turned red in England and Scotland just before the French revolution broke out, many thinking it was a sign of bloodshed to come. Although it rarely happens, the aurora tends to manifest itself in shades of red in the south of Europe, rather than green, like here." He looked around the group, his eyes wide with excitement. He was clearly passionate about the subject. "In Japan, many people believe that a child conceived under the northern lights will be lucky. That's why so many Japanese tourists visit the Arctic Circle during the aurora season. The aurora borealis has Galileo to thank for its name. He named the lights after the Roman goddess of the dawn and the Greek name for the wind. The oldest and most widely known myth comes from the Romans. They believed that Aurora, the goddess of dawn, was the sister of Helios, who was the sun, and Seline, who was the moon, and that she flew across the sky to let them know that a new day was coming." He pointed at the sky. "Look, it's starting."

Faint sparks manifested in the sky and everyone around the fire looked up, holding their breath, silently waiting for more to come. Werner and Charlotte got out of their seats, their heads turned up to the tiny spot where something seemed to be happening. Then, a luminous white glow appeared above the mountains in the distance. Kristine looked up, her eyes wide with anticipation. The glow spread towards them and slowly turned green. First, a subdued hue, then it turned brighter as the sky seemed to dance, taking on colored shapes rather than being uniform.

Captured in awe, everyone suddenly lowered their voices, respectful of the heavenly spectacle before them.

"Wow," Kristine whispered. She reached for Hannah's hand and intertwined their fingers. Hannah didn't resist. "I can see why people believed the northern lights to be some sort of God."

"This is magical," Hannah whispered back, transfixed by the sky. She couldn't have prepared herself for this and she felt a lump in her throat and tears welling up. She pointed skyward, surprised at her emotional reaction. "Look, it's taking on the shape of a heart."

"It is." Kristine took a picture. "You can see more colors on the photographs. The colors that our eyes don't detect. Look." She lowered her phone and showed the image to Hannah as she moved her cheek close to hers.

"Wow." Hannah tried to focus on the photograph, which was indeed beautiful, but Kristine's lips so close to hers made it very hard.

"No more phone now." Kristine said, lightly brushing her lips against Hannah's cheek before she turned away. She dropped the phone into her bag and sank back in her chair. "I shouldn't be looking through a lens. This is a once in a lifetime experience and I just want to enjoy it." She paused. "With you."

Hannah averted her eyes from the dazzling lightshow, locking her eyes with Kristine's. She wanted to make sure she'd heard her right. A stir of arousal flared deep in her core when she saw Kristine's flirty smile and, immediately, her lips pulled into a smile too. She distractedly ran a finger over her cheek, where Kristine's lips had been only seconds ago. *Holy shit.* She was usually the one doing the flirting, but Kristine definitely seemed to be turning the tables on her, and it took Hannah a few moments to get her natural charm back. Kristine looked even more beautiful under the mystical light, sparks from the flickering fire reflecting in her eyes. Her face was glowing with excitement, or maybe it was a blush. Either way, she didn't shy away. Her sun-bleached hair fell around her shoulders, the edges glowing green from the aurora. Hannah wasn't sure if it was the wine or the northern lights, but she was mesmerized by the sight of Kristine, and most of all, she felt connected to her. *She looks like a Nordic goddess.* Hannah bit her lip, fighting the urge to claim Kristine's mouth right there and then. She was sure no one was watching them. Everyone else was too busy with their phones and cameras, completely absorbed by the aurora.

"Not here," Kristine whispered, reading Hannah's mind. "Later." She'd been thinking about it all night, about how it would feel to kiss Hannah, and she needed it more than anything now. But there was no rush and she wanted whatever was going on between them to stay private. She took Hannah's hand again as they watched the spectacle unfolding in the sky that was now filled with green and turquoise patterns, slowly spreading out, creating a dome over the Earth. Then they started drooping down, like icicles far above the white lake. A bright white light appeared, a starburst, thousands of miles away.

Hannah felt lifted by something big, something incredibly powerful that was much greater than herself and for a moment, she understood things that were normally beyond her understanding. She even felt that, for a split second, she could grasp what was truly important in life, frozen in a state of peace and wonderment. There was an almost tangible silence amongst their group during the following hour. A few were whispering, but most were quietly staring up at the sky, even after the lights had subsided.

"Wow. That was..." Kristine fell silent as she finally turned to Hannah.

"I know." Hannah only then realized that her hand was still locked with Kristine's. She gave it a squeeze before Kristine squeezed her hand back, as if confirming they had experienced something incredible together, something that distance or time could never take away from them. "I'm happy I saw this with you," she whispered. "I was silly not to expect much. I guess I underestimated how powerful Mother Nature can be."

"I wouldn't have wanted to watch it with anyone else in the world." Kristine took off her glove and reached out to touch Hannah's cheek. She had a sparkle in her eyes and it was so infectious, it made Hannah smile herself.

"I'm going to bed," Hannah whispered, covering Kristine's hand with her own. It felt warm and wonderful against her cheek, silky soft like the touch of an angel. She looked around the campfire. Their fellow group members were talking louder now, and soon they would need something else to focus on, now that the lights were gone.

"Wait... I'm coming," Kristine said in a soft voice, retracting her hand. She stood up and locked her eyes with Hannah's. Hannah's stomach did crazy things as her mind went to places she couldn't quite handle. "I think I'm tired too." Kristine's words didn't sound in the least convincing and, by the look on her face, she was wide awake.

"Okay." Hannah turned to the group. "Goodnight guys. I had the most amazing night. Happy Christmas." The reply was loud and cheerful, as if they were all best friends already.

"Goodnight," Kristine added, waving at them.

"Are you really tired?" Hannah studied Kristine and felt a tingle of excitement at her dark expression when she held open the door to the hotel. "We could have a nightcap in my room if you want?" She removed her jacket and hung it on the rack on the wall in the hallway, then she helped Kristine out of her jacket and hung it over her own. There was a strange intimacy in that simple gesture. She liked the idea of Kristine's scent rubbing off on her jacket. Kristine turned to her after she'd removed her shoes.

"No, I'm not tired." She paused and shot Hannah another glance that made her weak at the knees. "But I'm pretty sure you're well aware of that. A *nightcap* would be nice." Kristine lowered her voice when she articulated the word, making sure Hannah knew exactly what she wanted. They walked up the stairs in silence, both very aware of the sizzling attraction between them that seemed to have multiplied after their already magical night.

"Do you mind if we go to my room instead?" Kristine asked when they had reached the first-floor landing. She shuffled on the spot, her confidence suddenly crumbling a little when she realized she hadn't done what they were about to do in a very long time, and she wanted to be comfortable and in her own space. "It's just that..." Her voice trailed away.

"Of course not," Hannah whispered, noticing her sudden change in demeanor. "It's fine. Let's go to yours." She waited for Kristine to open the door to her room, then followed her inside. Kristine crossed the room with trembling legs, switching on the lights of the Christmas tree; the action giving her the opportunity to take a deep breath. Then she lit the three red tapered candles situated on each nightstand. The flames cast a warm glow over the wall, blending in perfectly with the subtle lights on the tree. *What was I thinking flirting with her like that? Now she's going to think I'm some kind of vixen in bed and I don't even know what I'm doing.*

"You're tidy," Hannah remarked, taking in the room. There were no clothes strewn across the floor and no empty water bottles or used mugs on the nightstand. "Not messy, like me." Just like her own room, Kristine's room was cozy and warm, decorated with traditional Norwegian patterns, woodwork and a Christmassy throw over the sofa by the window. The thick black and white rug that covered most of the wooden floor was almost identical too, apart from the pattern.

"Yeah. I like to keep things in order." They stood there for a couple of seconds, staring at each other. "I don't normally do this," Kristine suddenly blurted out. "With someone I don't know very well." She shot Hannah a nervous glance. "Hell, I don't normally do this at all. It's been... I don't know... years, I guess." She walked over to the window and closed the drapes.

"That's okay." Hannah took a step towards her, closing the distance between them. She took Kristine's face in her hands. "Hey, we don't have to do this. We can just have a cup of tea and I'll go back to my own room. Just because we're attracted to each other doesn't mean we have to do anything."

"No. I want to." Kristine let out a sigh. "I don't think I've ever wanted anything as much as I want you right now." She placed her own hands over Hannah's and closed her eyes. "I never meet women that I like. I never feel that spark, you know?" She paused. "But I feel it now and it's stronger than I ever imagined."

"I feel it too." Hannah traced Kristine's cheeks with her thumbs. Her skin felt soft under her fingertips. She gave Kristine a reassuring smile. "This is new to me too, in a way.

I'm not at some party, looking to score and leave the same night. I'm fairly sober and I know you'll be here tomorrow and the coming days. There's no going back or avoiding each other if we do this." She leaned in. "But I want you and I can see that you want me too. So we'll take it slow. Really slow." She studied Kristine's face. The blue eyes that mesmerized her each time she looked into them, the faint dimples in her cheeks, the few freckles strewn across her face, and the fullness of her lips. "God, you're so beautiful, Kristine." Hannah brushed her lips against Kristine's and kissed her softly, shivering at the rush she felt. Kristine's mouth was perfect in every way, just like she'd imagined.

Kristine answered her kiss with a soft moan, parting her lips as she pulled Hannah in, taking off her beanie, before throwing it on the floor. She ran a hand through Hannah's silky hair and gave in to the overwhelming sensation of their tongues colliding, her nerves calming as the raging hormones took over. *This feels insane.* She hesitantly pulled out of the kiss, only to slide the straps of her padded snowsuit off her shoulders, before letting Hannah strip her out of her turtleneck top. The room was warm, the radiator blasting, and her body was steaming from the kiss. Slow or not, she really needed at least some of her clothes off.

Hannah smiled, her eyes filled with desire, as she lifted Kristine's black vest top over her head, revealing a black lace bra. She traced the edge of Kristine's bra around her back, making goose bumps appear on Kristine's arms. Her breasts were full, compared to her slim frame, and soft like velvet. "I've never undressed anyone who had so many layers of clothing on," she said in a teasing tone, unhooking Kristine's bra with one hand. She used her other hand to trace Kristine's waist down to her snowsuit that was still hanging low on her hips. "But we've got all night."

Kristine felt more at ease now. She allowed Hannah to take off her bra, exposing her breasts. Her nipples were hard, her breasts aching to be touched. Hannah ran a hand over them as their mouths met again in another passionate kiss that made Kristine's last reservations melt like snow.

"Take this off," she said through ragged breaths, looking at Hannah's snowsuit. Her eyes were full of need, all the years of longing now cultivated into a perverse urge to ravage Hannah. She tugged at the shoulder straps and slid them down before lifting the hem of Hannah's woolen sweater, taking off her t-shirt underneath in the process too. She let them drop onto the floor, her eyes fixed on Hannah's slim, athletic body and her hard nipples showing through her sheer bra. Her lips parted, mesmerized at the sight of Hannah, half undressed. As if pulled by a magnetic force, they fell into another kiss, both moaning at the electric chemistry that was stratospheric. Hannah's hands ran down the sides of Kristine's body before she hooked her thumbs inside her snowsuit pants, tugging them over her hips until they fell down. Kristine stepped out of them without breaking the kiss. She did the same to Hannah, impatiently yanking at the suit until Hannah helped her and pulled it down herself, along with her thermal leggings.

"You feel so good," Kristine mumbled into the kiss. Their warm bodies finally coming together was almost too much to handle. Kristine felt Hannah's hands sink inside the back of her leggings, covering her ass and squeezing it as she pulled her closer, their hips and breasts pressed against each other. "Oh God." She closed her eyes, savoring the warm mouth that was claiming her as if they were the last two people left on Earth. She trailed a fingertip over Hannah's small breast, drawing a soft moan from her.

Hannah pulled out of the kiss, staring at Kristine with a

mystified expression on her face. "Wow..." she whispered. "I didn't expect this to be so..." She didn't finish her sentence.

"Yeah." Kristine said softly, locking her eyes with Hannah's. She was breathing fast, her chest heaving up and down with excitement and anticipation as she pulled down her leggings and her panties and stepped out of them. She looked from the rug by the Christmas tree to the king-size bed and back.

"Rug," Hannah said with a mischievous smile.

"Good call." Kristine lowered herself onto the thick rug and looked up at Hannah. The lights from the Christmas tree and the flickering candles illuminated Hannah's pale skin. They made her look like a dark angel when she ran a hand through her hair, that was still messy from the beanie she'd been wearing since breakfast that morning. Her tiny black lace panties brought a surprisingly sexy twist to her tomboy appearance and her eyes were dark and mysterious, twinkling with desire as she got down on her knees before Kristine and slowly lowered herself on top of her. She shifted a thigh between Kristine's legs and pushed it against her center while she kissed her hard and deep, unable to hold back despite her promise to go slow.

Kristine closed her eyes and moaned at the contact. She ran a trembling hand over Hannah's back, tracing her spine upwards towards her neck, lacing her fingers through her silky hair. It had been so long since she'd been intimate with a woman that she'd almost forgotten how good it felt. But being with Hannah was beyond her wildest dreams. She threw her head back into the soft rug when Hannah's mouth shifted to her neck, kissing her sensitive skin. When Hannah grabbed her thigh, she bent her knee and lifted her hips a little so that Hannah's other hand could move onto her ass.

Hannah inhaled deep against Kristine's tanned skin as she kissed her way down to her breasts. Her body lotion smelt like honey; sweet and pure. It felt elevating, almost surreal as if she was looking down on herself while she made Kristine moan in pleasure. The northern lights, and the beautiful setting they found themselves in, had drawn them into a fairy tale, yet the connection she felt to Kristine was so strong and real, that her body ached to consume all of her. Hannah pressed her lips against a pink, hard nipple, her mouth pulling into a smile at Kristine's gasp. She was so responsive and so sensual in her movements, the way she arched her back and circled her hips as if in some kind of trance-like state. Hannah bit down gently, letting her tongue run over the tip.

"Fuck, Hannah! Yes!" Kristine arched her back, raising her chest against Hannah's mouth.

Hannah smiled as she scraped her teeth over Kristine's skin and kissed her way down to her belly. She then let her tongue run down to the soft hairline between her legs. Kristine rolled her hips against Hannah's chest and Hannah felt Kristine's wetness against her breasts. *Oh my God, she wants me. She really wants me.* She stayed there, teasing Kristine with her tongue, before she traced the inside of her thighs.

"Oh God!" Kristine covered her face with her hands, dampening her moans when Hannah spread her legs and traced her folds with her tongue. The arousal in her lower abdomen stirred like a storm that was about to turn into a hurricane. "You're killing me," she said in a whimper. Hannah's face pulled into a grin at her words as she tasted Kristine and heard her moan in pleasure. She let her tongue run over Kristine's sex again, resting it on her clit, pressing down harder this time.

"That feels amazing!" Kristine wiggled underneath her, squirming in ecstasy. "Not yet," she begged.

But Hannah couldn't wait. She was too caught up in the moment, too eager to make Kristine come. She circled her tongue around Kristine's clit, slow at first, then faster as she reached up to caress her breasts. Kristine held her breath, trying to make the build-up last. It was more powerful than anything she'd ever felt and she wanted to remember it. Hannah could sense she was close, and she carefully entered her with two fingers, still stimulating her clit with her tongue. She wanted to feel Kristine's orgasm and she wanted to be as close as she possibly could when she exploded.

"Yes!" Kristine arched her back again and buried her face in her hands, desperately trying to stifle the screams that were about to leave her mouth. She grabbed Hannah's hair and pushed her mouth harder against her center, shutting her eyes tight as waves of pleasure washed over her.

Hannah moaned against Kristine's center when she felt her contractions twitch around her fingers and her body shake in delight. She looked up to watch Kristine's face as she lost herself in the moment. Her lips parted, and her eyelashes fluttered, her expression entranced.

Kristine trembled long after she'd peaked, surprised at the heavenly orgasm that had just taken over her. *What the hell just happened?* She wiped her forehead that was beaded with sweat and tried to catch her breath as she looked up at Hannah, who was now on top of her, placing a trail of warm kisses down her neck.

"Hmm..." she moaned. "God, you sure know what you're doing, Hannah."

Hannah smiled, kissing her way back up Kristine's neck to her jaw and finally meeting her mouth. Kristine wrapped her arms around Hannah and pulled her as close as she could while they shared a passionate kiss.

"I don't know about that." Hannah grinned. "Maybe you're just easy to please."

Kristine sat up and pushed Hannah down into the rug, hovering above her. Hannah was so goddamn sexy, that even after what had just happened, it still all seemed like a dream. She was simply too good to be true.

"Or maybe you're just really, really talented... No pressure on me." Kristine traced Hannah's upper lip with her tongue, drawing a moan from her mouth. She moved her hand down Hannah's torso, finally allowing herself to look at her the way she'd wanted to for days. She took her time, watching Hannah move underneath her touch. When her fingers skimmed the elastic of Hannah's panties, she wiggled them inside and grinned when she saw her face pull into an expression of pure delight. The first soft touch of her fingers on Hannah's center made her gasp and close her eyes. Kristine watched her as she bit her bottom lip, and it was then that she realized that she had her, even if it was just for tonight. The gorgeous and trendy London girl was completely at her mercy and she wanted nothing more than to be touched by her. She moved her fingers down, teasingly slow. Hannah grabbed a handful of the rug and bucked her hips, begging for more. Her other hand was in Kristine's hair, pulling her down into a kiss. Kristine sank into her mouth, marveling at the knowledge that she was the cause of Hannah's pleasure. She felt Hannah's wetness, her urge for release, and when she entered her, the world around them faded away. They were one.

"Kristine..." Hannah whispered through ragged breaths. "Yes, like that..." Kristine smiled when she knew that she was balancing on the edge. She kissed her again, with more urgency this time, draping herself over Hannah's warm skin as she penetrated her deeper, holding her fingers still when Hannah's gasp told her she'd hit the spot. She felt Hannah's climax as if it were her own. The pleasure was all the same, that she was sure of. As she pulled out of the kiss, and watched her buckle beneath her, Kristine felt a sense of togetherness that almost made her burst into tears. Hannah held onto her, digging her nails into her back and for the first time in her life, Kristine felt needed.

"You're amazing, Hannah," she whispered as Hannah closed her eyes and started to relax.

"You told me you're not in contact with your family," Kristine said cautiously. She felt the need, a real need, to get to know Hannah better but she didn't want to scare her off by coming across as nosy. They were seated on the balcony and it was cold despite the two heaters. They had three blankets over their legs and the thick comforter from the bed draped around them, their bodies still naked underneath. The night was so beautiful that she'd suggested sitting outside for a little while, after they'd had a shower together. The campfire below was almost out, just a few embers left in the pile of ash, and it was so quiet that she could hear the ice on the lake cracking in the distance. She felt relaxed and blissfully happy, after indulging in Hannah's body for hours on end. Hannah was an amazing lover, there was no doubt about that. But their chemistry was something entirely different. Just the touch of Hannah's arm against hers under the covers was enough to arouse her again. She leaned her head on her shoulder, pulling the comforter under her chin. "Do you have any brothers or sisters?" she carefully continued. Thin slivers of green were still hanging in the sky, the goddess Aurora slowly retracting from the Earth's atmosphere.

"I was adopted," Hannah said after a long silence. "I didn't tell you because I didn't want you to feel sorry for me. I spent most of my life with foster families, so no, I don't have any siblings. Not that I know of, anyway." She pulled Kristine closer and shot her a reassuring glance. "I'm okay though. I'm happy and I'm proud of what I've achieved, all on my own. My friends are my family and my restaurant is my life. That's all I need."

"I'm sorry to hear that." There was no pity in Kristine's voice. "Where you born in the UK?"

"Yes. All I know is that my birth mother was English and I was adopted at birth. I don't remember my adoptive parents but I've been told they died during an accident when I was two years old. Their family didn't want to take care of me, so I was put into foster care." She shook her head, staring into nothing. "My birth records were kept private until I was sixteen but I never felt the need to look my mother up even when I was old enough. I didn't care about finding her. She gave me away like a thing, like it didn't matter to her what sort of life I would have, leaving me to move from foster family to foster family, finally ending up with this awful couple who only wanted more children so they could claim extra benefits." She paused. "That was the only reason they adopted me, when I was ten. Because they didn't have to look after me, or so they thought. From the moment I moved in, I was the one cleaning the house, doing the cooking and running to the night shop at eleven every night to get more beer because they weren't drunk enough. That was the only life I knew for as long as I lived with them. So, when I was about sixteen, I decided I'd had enough and I moved in with my first girlfriend. She was studying English and I lived in her student room. I got my first job serving coffee at a café and, although our relationship didn't last very long, we carried on living together and we're still best friends. The day I moved out was the last time I saw my last foster parents and I have no intention of ever seeking contact again. I was the youngest, so I didn't worry too much about the two boys who were still living there. We never got along, and besides, they were already well on their way to becoming petty criminals. I figured they could take care of themselves."

"That must have been harsh for you, being that young. You were lucky to have a place to go. Imagine, you could have been living on the streets if your friend hadn't let you live with her." Kristine pressed her lips against Hannah's temple.

"Yeah. Mandy saved me, in a way. We still see each other once a week. She's got two kids now with her wife Annabel. They're gorgeous and I'm a proud godmother to them both." She smiled, covering Kristine's hand with her own. "How about you? Tell me about your family."

Kristine was silent for a moment. "I feel uncomfortable complaining about our family dynamics after what you've just told me. I'm only going to sound spoilt."

"No. Please tell me." Hannah said. "I want to know more about you."

"Okay..." Kristine paused again. "Well... I have two brothers as I told you, Joe and Jed. They're fruit farmers, since they have each taken over half of my parents' farm after my father hurt his back. Both Joe and Jed, as well as my father, are as hard-headed as mules and not the brightest men around. They fight over everything, from money to business matters, to the shoes that they're wearing. Get them together in a room and you'll be sure to have a near fistfight within the hour. My mother has no say in anything. She's just the farmer's wife and she chose to settle in that role the day she married my father. She works harder than any of them but gets little or no credit, let alone any gratefulness for everything she does for them. And then there's me. I managed to get a scholarship and went off to university. I studied finance, only to piss my father off, if I may add." She let out a chuckle. "And now they think I'm a snob because I run a bank. Joe got furious with me two years ago when I told him I couldn't just give him a loan to expand his side of the farm. He seems to be under the impression that I can just open a safe and hand him a batch of money without a business plan or a security deposit. And it's not even me deciding about the loans, we have a policy for that and I get audited. Anyway, I don't see them very often, even though we live close. I have coffee with my mother every week though. It's the only time she gets to speak her mind and when she does, she just keeps ranting about my father."

"Sounds like you've got your hands full with them." Hannah laughed.

"Yeah well, as I said it's nothing compared to what you've been through and it's really not that bad. I just ignore them in general."

"Does your family know you're gay?" Hannah asked.

"They know. But they're not happy about it. I've never even wanted to bring a girlfriend home, I'm just not that close to them. They'd probably have a heart attack. Not that I've ever met a woman I wanted to bring home."

"Have you not been in any long-term relationships?" Hannah tucked a strand of loose hair behind Kristine's ear and softly kissed behind it.

"A couple. Most of them in my early twenties. But not in the past seven or eight years, no. I've become a lot pickier, since I've grown up. I don't want to waste my time anymore with one-night stands, or flings that will never work out."

She laughed when Hannah shot her a skeptical look. "Apart from tonight, of course. This was most certainly not a waste of time.... And I know I'll never regret it." She looked at Hannah. "I'm thirty-five, in case you're wondering." She sighed. "Not getting any younger."

"Come on. You're beautiful." Hannah nudged her. "I can't stop looking at you, haven't you noticed? You caught my interest since the first day we met."

"Oh yeah?" Kristine shot her a smile. "I felt the same way when I first saw you. There's something dark and mysterious about you that's incredibly intriguing. That, and you're beautiful. I've never met anyone like you before." She studied Hannah. "So, how old are you?"

"Thirty-three. My birthday was last week."

"Really?" Kristine narrowed her eyes. "You look younger and your skin is flawless." She traced the back of her hand over Hannah's cheek, down to her neck and around her back as she pulled her in for a kiss. Hannah shifted closer and ran a hand through Kristine's hair, moaning softly. Lost in their kiss, they forgot about the comforter, the material slipping off their shoulders as they moved.

"Damn, it's cold," Hannah exclaimed, breaking their kiss. She shivered as she pulled the comforter back over them. "Shall we go back inside? Warm each other up in bed?"

"Yeah. Let's go. I wasn't ready to stop kissing you but it's a little complicated trying to stay warm when it's freezing outside." Kristine giggled as they stood up and shuffled sideways towards the door together, wrapped up tight in the layers of wool and feathers. She yanked at the sliding door but there was no movement. "Shit, it's stuck." She tried again, unsuccessfully.

"Let me give it a go." Hannah shuffled them around in a

circle, their bodies still pressed together, so she was now at the door. She tried to pull it open while Kristine secured the blankets. "I don't think it's stuck," she said after several attempts. "I think it's locked itself." She looked worried for a moment but couldn't suppress a chuckle.

Kristine laughed too. "Jesus. What are we going to do? We can't start screaming, right? Everyone will know what we've been up to. I mean, look at us."

"I don't think we've got a choice." Hannah shrugged. "Hey, it's not a big deal. We're adults and we haven't done anything wrong. The worst that can happen is that we'll be a bit embarrassed but we'll live." She put an arm around Kristine's waist and pulled her closer. Kristine's pubic hair was tickling her hip and she fought to stay focused on getting them out of there instead of pushing Kristine against the door and kissing her again. She took a deep breath, thinking for a moment. "Okay, they've all had a fair bit to drink, so everyone's probably fast asleep by now, apart from Dani, who's pregnant. Dani and Espen's apartment is on the other side of the building but if we're lucky she'll hear us. Or maybe your neighbors, Sofia and Gunnar will but they both seemed pretty drunk tonight. We've got to do this together. It needs to be loud, okay?"

"Okay..." Kristine wasn't too convinced, but she didn't have a better idea either, so she nodded. "I'll count to three. One... two... three... Help!" they screamed in unison. They waited for a couple of seconds, trying to detect any sign of life in the hotel. Then they screamed again. "Help!"

After a lengthy silence they heard a sliding sound. The balcony door of the adjoining room then opened.

"Hello? Is everything alright?" Gunnar's voice sounded cracked. They heard his slippers shuffle on the balcony before his head peeked over the wall. "Oh... hi ladies." He frowned, gazing at Kristine and Hannah, wrapped up in the blankets. "What the hell are you two doing out here in the cold?"

"Thank God you woke up, Gunnar. Looks like we've managed to lock ourselves out," Kristine said. "And it's really cold." She gestured at the door. "I don't think the door to my room is locked. Would you mind letting us back in? And if it's locked, could you please ask Dani for the spare key?"

Gunnar scratched his bald head with a suspicious look on his face. "Sure. I'll be right there."

A few moments later, Gunnar was in Kristine's room, unlocking the balcony door. He stared at them as they tried to make their way inside, face to face, shuffling sideways.

"We were cold," Hannah said with a grateful smile. "Just trying to keep warm, Gunnar. Body heat is the key, I've been told."

"Right. Yes, of course." Gunnar's cheeks flared red as he spotted their bare legs underneath the blankets. "I'd better get back then." He walked out of the room as fast as his old legs would carry him.

"Thank you so much!" Kristine yelled after him. "I think you might have saved our lives!"

## 9

## THE MORNING AFTER

"Morning," Hannah whispered after she'd switched off the alarm on her phone. "And Merry Christmas."

Kristine looked confused at first. She blinked a couple of times before the memories came flooding back. Then she gave Hannah a big smile and scooted closer, wrapping an arm around her waist.

"Merry Christmas, Hannah. What a nice surprise to see you're still here."

"I hope you don't mind," Hannah whispered, pulling Kristine in as she buried her face in her hair. The sensation of their bodies pressed together had aroused her instantly and she couldn't suppress a moan when Kristine nestled a thigh between her legs.

"Not at all. It's a welcome surprise. I just didn't take you for the sleepover type."

Kristine was right. Hannah wasn't the sleepover type, at least she hadn't been lately. She usually left as soon as she got the chance, sometimes lying awake for hours until her latest conquest had finally fallen asleep, so that she could sneak out quietly. But as her body had entwined with Kristine's last night it had felt so natural, and so good, that she hadn't wanted to leave.

"Maybe I like sharing a bed with you," she said in a playful tone as she squeezed Kristine's ass. Kristine was beautiful and deliciously sexy, especially now, with her hair tousled and a big grin on her face. She felt butterflies in her belly at the sight of her and an overwhelming urge to press closer, something that hadn't happened to her in a very long time. She kissed Kristine softly, tugging her into a tender embrace. Kristine's quiet moans fired her up, bringing her body back to life in only a few seconds. Her hands started leading a life of their own, exploring the velvet touch of Kristine's skin and stroking her silky soft hair.

"Stop," Kristine said, pulling out of the kiss, breathing fast. "You're making me crave you all over again." She slowly sat up and looked at her phone. "It's almost nine. They'll be wondering where we are, gossiping over breakfast if we don't show up."

"I know," Hannah whispered, running a finger down Kristine's breasts and stomach before pulling her back in. "But you're here, and I'm here and as it happens we're both naked, so..." Her focus shifted to Kristine's full breasts. They were perfect. She folded her lips around a hard nipple and caressed it with her tongue. Kristine gasped and shifted her hips towards her, clearly just as aroused as Hannah was.

"Ten or twenty minutes isn't going to make a difference," Hannah continued in a flirty tone. "Imagine how we could put that time to use..."

10

## CHRISTMAS DAY

"Good morning ladies and Merry Christmas," Sofia said as Hannah and Kristine walked into the dining room. Her curiosity was almost palpable. The tables were still in the same position as the night before, creating one big dining table, and there was nowhere to hide.

"Merry Christmas," Hannah and Kristine mumbled awkwardly, to nobody in particular. Then they took the two empty seats in the middle of the table opposite each other, both trying to avoid the eight pairs of eyes that were now staring at them as the room fell silent.

"I heard you locked yourselves out last night," Sofia continued in her high-pitched voice. "We heard screaming and I sent Gunnar out to see what was going on. He told me he found you both locked out on the balcony. He must have saved you from freezing to death." She proudly rubbed her husband's shoulder. "Poor girls. You must have been so scared."

"Yeah, he definitely saved us." Hannah looked at Gunnar, who was clearly mortified by his wife's need to inform the whole group about the embarrassing episode. He looked up and smiled but avoided her eyes. "Thank you again, Gunnar. I don't know what would have happened without you."

"No problem ladies," he mumbled, focusing on his scrambled eggs.

"So, what were you doing out there in the freezing cold wearing nothing but a couple of blankets?" Sarah asked. "Sofia told us you were naked." Hannah shot Sarah a sharp look, but she continued her interrogation, oblivious. *Of course it had to be Sarah.* "I mean, the northern lights were long gone and it was at least minus four."

Werner and Charlotte burst into laughter, clearly aware of what had been going on.

"Eh... we were stargazing," Kristine tried. "I'm a naturist, so I like to feel at one with Mother Nature while I observe her... eh..." Hannah kicked her leg under the table but couldn't manage to suppress a grin as her eyes locked with Josh's, who was fighting his own urge to laugh, clearly more switched on than his wife.

"Wonders," she finished Kristine's sentence. "We were paying our respect to Mother Nature's wonders and didn't realize we'd locked the balcony door."

Dani came out of the kitchen with fresh coffee, saving them from Sarah's annoying questions.

"You guys okay?" she asked. "I heard you got locked out. I'm so sorry I didn't hear you; since I've been pregnant I sleep like the dead. Anyway, I'm glad Gunnar rescued you. Imagine..." She shook her head. "We really need to replace those doors."

"No, it's fine," Hannah reassured her. "It was just a stupid mistake. Won't happen again."

"I wish my wife would lock us out every now and then,"

Werner joked. He flinched when Charlotte kicked him under the table. Hannah wanted to hug Dani, who tried to change the subject by making small talk and refilling everyone's coffee mugs. When there was nothing left for her to do, and she'd run out of things to talk about, she called Espen into the dining room.

"God Jul, everyone," Espen appeared after a couple of minutes, looking sleepy and a little rough. But he smiled broadly and was clearly in good spirits, sipping from his coffee mug as he looked around the table. "Anyone up for cross-country skiing today? A bit of exercise to work off all the food and alcohol we consumed last night?"

"Absolutely," Josh said.

"We're in. We're loving the daily exercise," Charlotte shouted from across the table.

"Great. For those of you who have never tried skiing before, it's not that hard," Espen added. "The first four miles are flat, so you'll have plenty of time to get into it. Then we'll climb for a mile before we go downhill for the last mile. There are tracks going down, so that will make it easier."

"I'm not sure if my back can handle it," Sofia said. "It's still a little sore from the hike earlier in the week. I think I'm getting old."

"Don't worry Sofia, we'll take care of you." Espen patted her on the shoulder, then turned to the others. "As mentioned in your itineraries, we're going to ski over to the ice-hotel and enjoy Christmas lunch there. They do great king crab. It's a specialty around here. In fact, Norway have the best king crab in the world." He winked at Gunnar. "We Norwegians have the best in the world of everything, although the Danish don't always agree. For those of you who don't feel like skiing today, you can do the dishes." He laughed. "Just kidding. Enjoy yourselves around the fire and relax. We have lots of board games if you prefer to exercise your brains rather than your limbs. If any of you don't want to ski to the ice-hotel, Dani can drive you over later and we'll meet you there. We'll also drive you all back. The ice-hotel will provide a second van. Twelve miles of skiing in a day is too much, even for me. Besides that, it will be pitch dark by the time we finish lunch and we don't want to get lost in the woods."

"Are you up for skiing?" Kristine whispered, when the diners around them seemed distracted enough not to listen in on their conversation. Hannah watched her stir sugar into her coffee, looking adorable as she tried to wake up. Their lovemaking only an hour ago had been sleepy and slow, but also so sensual and sexy as hell. Hannah shifted in her chair as she thought of it, sipping her coffee.

"Absolutely." Hannah paused. "That is, if you are. I want to spend time with you, so I'll go wherever you go... Unless you're sick of me by now?"

Kristine grinned. "No way I'm sick of you. How could I be?" She cocked her head. "I'm only just starting to get used to you, so you'd better brace yourself for the coming days."

"You have no idea what you're getting yourself into," Hannah teased.

"I think I have a pretty good idea," Kristine shot back at her. "And I happen to like it. A lot."

"Do you always bring your rifle along?" Charlotte asked in her heavy German accent when Espen slung a rifle over his shoulder. They were getting into their snowsuits and snow boots in the hallway, grabbing onto anything in sight as they tried to keep their balance.

"Yup. We're pretty remote here," he said. "And it's a good six miles to the hotel. We need to be prepared for anything, and by anything, I mean animals, mainly. I don't worry too much about the Russians." He laughed loudly at his own joke. "Wolves, bears, elks..." He paused for dramatic effect. "Especially elks, can be very dangerous when they're angry, even if you're in a car. I've never had to kill an animal out there and I hope I never will, but if it's me or them, I like to make sure I have the upper hand."

Hannah grinned and held on to his shoulder as she balanced on one leg, tugging at her snow boot. "In that case, I'm glad you're here to protect us," she said.

"Me too," Kristine nodded in agreement. "I'm so excited. Every time we go outside it feels like a brand-new adventure." She bit her bottom lip. "But I've never attempted to stand on a pair of skis in my life, so I sincerely hope I won't slow y'all down."

"We'll take it slow," Espen reassured her. "And cross-country skiing isn't that hard, you'll get the hang of it in no time."

The air was crisp as Hannah and Kristine were slowly gliding downhill, relieved that the long, steep climb was over. It wasn't difficult, but the sideways hike up the mountain had been tiring, and now it felt like a reward to clumsily slide down the mountain, following the marks Espen had made in the snow. Everyone was able to keep up so far and only Sofia and Gunnar had stayed behind with Dani. Sofia because of her back, and Gunnar most likely because of last night's heavy drinking and their balcony incident after that. Hannah still found that funny, even though she felt a bit guilty for his trauma at seeing two naked women entangled in blankets together.

Hannah had never attempted to ski herself, but she was starting to get the hang of it now, and she was enjoying it. Kristine – whom she now knew to be highly competitive – was only a few feet in front of her. Their surroundings were beautiful and every now and then she stopped to take a picture, making sure Kristine was somewhere in the background. She was desperate for something to remember her by. Her legs were getting tired but there was no way she was going to give up, seeing Kristine speed up. Every now and then, they would all stop when someone – including herself – toppled over, but in general, her fellow group members seemed surprisingly steady on their feet. Hannah felt her hopes rise as she spotted something that looked like a building in the distance, or rather a group of buildings. The wooden domes, that were only just visible above snow level, looked like some secret lab from here. The main three-storey building next to the domes had a full glass wall on the top floor, facing a lake. Around it, as they neared it, strange shapes in the snow became visible too. Christmas lights were attached to a large fenced off area next to the main building, where reindeer were kept.

"Wow," Kristine said as she came to a halt next to Hannah. "This is amazing." Blue lights lit up the snow shapes that turned out to be hotel rooms. They could see the arched doorways now but, apart from that, there didn't seem to be any other building materials involved other than snow. The other wooden dome-shaped cabins that were built into the mountain blended into the scenery, covered in snow, apart from the facades which had a door and one large floor to ceiling window each, Christmas trees visible behind the glass.

"We're here." Espen removed his woolen hat and grinned as he steadied himself on his knees, trying to catch his breath. Clearly, last night's consumption of copious amounts of wine had taken its toll on him too.

"You okay?" Hannah asked.

"I am now." Espen straightened his back and led them to

the carport of the main building to store their skis and snowsuits, before climbing up the stairs to the restaurant. Once there, they were seated at a long table next to the floor to ceiling window that looked out over a white dreamscape. Kristine looked out through the window that was so polished, if it hadn't been for the heating that was on full blast, it would have felt like they were sitting outside. She reminded herself once again just how lucky she was to experience something like this, in a location she'd only ever dared to dream of before she came here.

"What a view." Josh spread out his arms, posing for a picture in front of the window.

"A little to the left, Josh," Sarah said. "And smile. You always look so awkward in pictures."

"I am smiling," Joshua defended himself. "What do you want from me? I don't know how else to look. You should know that, you married me."

Sarah sighed as she snapped a picture. "You've got to work on your camera face, Josh. Otherwise you'll look miserable in not only our wedding photos but in all our honeymoon pictures too."

"I think he looks handsome," Hannah helped him out, taking a seat next to Kristine. By now it was unthinkable that she'd sit anywhere else but by her side. She needed the closeness and, as the hours ticked away way too fast for her liking, she became aware that their time together was running out. She grinned as Kristine brushed a hand over her thigh under the table, and she placed her hand on top of it, keeping it there. She felt happier than she had in a long time after waking up next to Kristine. Even better, was that Beth walking out on her hadn't been the first thing on her mind since it'd happened. Instead, she'd been lying next to a beautiful woman who was not only kind and funny, but also charming in the cutest way and incredibly sexy. There was no awkwardness and there were no expectations between them. There was just the here and now, as they lived their temporary fairy tale in a dreamy landscape at the edge of the world. And she'd made her peace with that. Who cared if it wasn't real? Real things never worked out anyway. It was what it was, for as long as it lasted, and it was amazing. The curious looks they'd been getting from people in their group since breakfast that morning hadn't even annoyed her. Sofia especially seemed to be intrigued by them. But she didn't care what they thought and she didn't care that they knew. Right now, Kristine looked absolutely stunning with her long, blonde hair and stripped from her outerwear, left only in a tight black turtleneck, a black pair of leggings that made her ass irresistible, and her snow boots. Her full lips were shining with a hint of lip gloss and the blush on her cheeks, that Hannah now knew to be natural, was a light pink, highlighting her cheekbones.

"What is it?" Kristine asked, raising an eyebrow when she caught Hannah staring at her.

"You look delicious," Hannah whispered.

Kristine smiled broadly. "Thank you. So do you."

Josh, Sarah, Sofia and Gunnar were posing in front of the window together now, not paying them any attention. Dani and Espen were talking to the restaurant manager, ordering wine, while Werner and Charlotte were wandering around, admiring the canvases on the walls that had been painted by local artists.

In that exact moment, Kristine found herself in a fantasy, so real that she almost started believing in it. For a moment, they were a couple, and for a moment, she'd almost convinced herself it would last forever.

"It's really nice to be here with you," she said to Hannah in a soft voice.

Hannah's eyes were fixated on Kristine's lips, and she was dying to kiss her. "It is. It's beyond perfect." She hesitated. "I wish..."

"What?"

"I wish you didn't live so far away..." Hannah let her voice trail away and smiled. "But then if you didn't, you wouldn't have that cute accent."

"I could say the same for you." Kristine shot her a teasing look as she thickened her Southern drawl. "I love how you talk." She laughed, but then her face turned serious. "I love everything about you and, honestly, I'm dreading saying goodbye to you."

"Me too." Hannah reached out and ran a hand through Kristine's hair. "Let's try not to think about it. It would only ruin the short time we have left."

"You're right." Kristine waited for the waiter to fill her wineglass with white wine and held it up. "Merry Christmas, Hannah. Here's to the best Christmas I've ever had."

"Here we go," Espen said with a grin, as proud as if he'd caught the crabs himself. "King crab like you've never had it before." Each of the three plates that were put in front of them on the table had two enormous deep red king crabs on them, slices of lemon, homemade mayonnaise, melted salted butter and freshly baked loaves of white bread. There were also salads and bottles of white wine and water. "It might look simple, but don't underestimate the flavor, they're the best and freshest ingredients we get around here."

"There's nothing simple about this," Sarah said, snapping pictures of the feast on the table. "And what are these for?" She picked up a set of strange looking tools that were lying next to her plate.

"They're to eat the crab with," Espen said. "Here, let me show you how it's done." He reached over and took hold of one of the crab legs with both hands, squinting as he broke one of the joints. "They're quite hard to break. I asked the kitchen to serve them whole for those of you who have never eaten crab this way. Thought you might find it interesting. Give it a go," he continued. "Crab legs have four sections and three joints. All you need to do first is break them." Apart from Sofia and Gunnar, who ate crab regularly in Denmark, and Hannah, who occasionally served it in her restaurant, no one knew what they were doing. Espen watched in amusement while his guests focused on the crabs, clumsily breaking their joints. "Now", he said, picking up a big piece of leg, "We use this to open up the leg down the soft side. Take one of the bigger pieces, they're the easiest. If you ever want to do this at home and you don't have a crab zipper, you can use a normal fork. It's a little harder, but it will work." He showed them the fork-shaped tool and ran it across the length, opening the crab leg before folding it open, revealing the meat inside. He scooped it out with his fork, dressed it with lemon and put a dollop of mayonnaise on top.

"This is really, really good," Hannah said after taking her first bite. "It's very sweet, better than any crab I've ever tasted."

"It's the best in the world." Espen smiled and held up another tool that looked like a nutcracker. "This is a crab cracker. It's for the smaller pieces. You break the shell with it, then peel the pieces off. With smaller crabs some people use lobster forks or chopsticks to get the meat out but these are so big that we won't need them." He pointed to the body of the crab in front of him. "You can eat the dark meat as well but most people prefer the white meat. I personally love the dark meat, it's a bit fishier."

"Gee, you're a natural at that, Joshua," Sofia remarked as she watched Joshua open the legs for Sarah. "And I'm a pro."

"Thanks Sofia." Joshua smiled as he passed the meat on to Sarah. "Would you like me to do another one, pumpkin?"

Hannah shot Kristine, who was fighting with her crab leg, an amused look. "Would you like me to help you with that, pumpkin?" she whispered.

"BEFORE WE HEAD BACK to the hotel, or go to church for those of you who would like that, we're going to sample some local schnapps," Espen said after lunch. "In the ice-bar, so you can get the full experience. It's the best place to taste some of the finest Norwegian akevitt, it's good for the digestion. You'll have to put your snowsuits back on, it's a separate building, or rather an igloo, outside. Everyone happy with that?"

"Sounds great," Gunnar said with a grin. Gunnar liked his tipple, Hannah had noticed, and every time he indulged, his nose took on a dark shade of purple.

The ice-bar, true to its name, was made up entirely of ice, both inside and out. The bar itself was carved out of ice and so were the shelves, the benches and the barstools. Along the walls were the most outrageous ice sculptures Hannah had ever seen on display, carved with such precision and detail that they could easily have been mistaken for crystal. A Christmas playlist, currently on *Mary's Boy Child* by Bonney M, was playing from a wireless speaker behind the bar.

"Merry Christmas people," the bartender – a tall, blonde and handsome man greeted them. He lined up ten shot glasses in front of them, removing one after Dani whispered something to him in Norwegian. He then picked up a clear bottle containing a golden liquid from the shelves behind him, holding it up for them to see. There was no label. "This is akevitt," he said. "It's made of potato and grains and it's a bit like gin, just flavored with caraway instead of juniper berries. It's got around forty percent of alcohol in it." He grinned. "Take it or leave it. I made this one myself, so I can't be too sure." He filled the glasses up to the brim. "I have three different ones. The other two are flavored with dill and cardamom but if you're not a strong drinker, and only want to try one, this is the best one in my opinion." He turned to Sofia and Gunnar, whom he'd heard speaking Danish to each other. "I know the Danish won't agree with me but, out of all the Scandinavian countries, Norway is generally known to have the best akevitt with the most distinctive character and the deepest color hue due to the ageing process in our oak barrels." Gunnar grunted his disagreement in Danish and the bartender laughed and shook his head. "We usually drink akevitt at room temperature but as this is an ice-bar it's a little colder than usual." Hannah and Kristine gave each other a challenging look, ready to take on the shots.

"Are you sure that's a good idea, Josh?" Sarah's eyes widened when Josh picked up one of the glasses. "You're not very good with alcohol sweetie. Maybe you should leave it."

"It's just a shot, Sarah. Chill out, it won't kill me." Josh said as he put the glass to his lips.

Hannah, Kristine and Sofia, who had heard the exchange, stopped talking for a moment, shocked by the fact that Josh was finally standing up for himself. The silence only lasted for a moment or two, before they realized it would only be more awkward if they focused on him, so they continued their conversation randomly, making up a subject and going along with it, hoping to deflect Josh's uncharacteristic outburst. Sarah was quiet. She seemed to be brooding over the unexpected mutiny as she picked up a shot glass herself.

"Let's have a toast!" Espen yelled, holding up his glass. "Skål, as we say in Norway, cheers, Merry Christmas, God Jul and may you all have a great New Year too. I hope you've enjoyed your stay with us so far." He knocked back his akevitt and the others followed suit, wincing after swallowing down the strong, burning liquor.

"Sweet Jesus." Kristine slammed her glass back on the bar and shook her head. "That's seriously strong stuff." She leaned in close to Hannah and shot her a flirty look. "If I have any more of this I won't be held responsible for my actions. My mind has been consumed with flashbacks of last night all day and that shot hasn't helped."

Hannah felt her cheeks flush. "Maybe I should encourage you to drink more then," she said with a smirk.

"Maybe you should." Now it was Kristine's time to blush.

"Are you two lovebirds going to have another one with me?" Sofia asked, interrupting their moment. Both Hannah and Kristine stared at her, shocked at her sudden breakdown of inhibition. "I'm sorry." Sofia gave them an apologetic look but was unable to suppress a chuckle. "Did I embarrass you? I didn't mean to, it's just that it's not exactly a secret around here." She picked up the next three glasses from the bar and casually handed Hannah and Kristine one each as if they'd been talking about the weather. "Well?"

"Sure, thank you," Kristine stammered before she held up her glass in another toast.

"To young love." Sofia winked, making their interaction even weirder. The uncomfortable moment was broken by Sarah's cardboard villain voice.

"Are you seriously having another one, Josh?" she said, trying to snatch the glass out of his hand. It was too late though. Josh had already dodged her and downed it, and was now leaning against the bar with a sheepish grin, his eyes glassy. He looked very pleased with himself and blissfully happy.

"I feel a domestic coming," Sofia whispered conspiratorially.

"I think you might be right." Hannah swallowed hard, trying to rid herself of the burning sensation in her throat. The liquor was strong and the days she used to drink shots with her staff after work were long over. To their relief, the bartender beckoned them all to come closer before Sarah had a chance to start an argument with Josh. He informed them about the distilling process and about different kinds of Norwegian home brew, including cherry and plum wine. Kristine felt warm and mellow, and slightly tipsy too. She didn't take in a word that was being said, instead she was completely focused on Hannah, who looked gorgeous, chewing her lip as she concentrated on the presentation that she seemed genuinely interested in. Kristine had never had a crush like this and she was gladly surrendering to all the wonderful feelings that were now a part of her holiday affair, marveling at how amazing it was to be completely and utterly in awe of someone who reciprocated her feelings of lust, knowing they had another steamy night ahead. Hannah was a by far the most fascinating and attractive woman she'd ever come across and she wasn't going to waste a minute apart from her while they were here.

"I'll have to get a couple of bottles for my restaurant,"

Hannah said when they left the ice-bar, following Espen and Dani to their car. "I love the flavor and I like the idea of a clear bottle without a label, although I'd have to find out if it's legal in the UK to sell it like that. I think I might be able to start a new trend in London. It's only natural that people will turn towards niche spirits, now that the whole beer homebrewing trend has skyrocketed." She gave Kristine a smug look. "And I'll be the first."

"Good thinking." Kristine nudged her. "You're fully in restaurant mode now by the way. You realize that, right?"

Hannah rolled her eyes. "Yeah, there's no escaping. I guess I'm just unable to switch off after all. At least I managed a good twenty-four hours, or maybe I was just too tired to think when I first got here."

"Seems to me like it's a good thing," Kristine said. "Your restaurant is your life, right? Your passion? Why would you want to switch off from that? I wish I loved my job that much." She laughed. "But that's certainly never going to happen."

"What would you do instead?" Hannah asked. "If you could make a switch tomorrow, what would your dream job be?"

"I don't know." Kristine was silent for a moment. "I love growing things, but I wouldn't want to go into farming on a bigger scale, like my family does. I've thought about it a lot over the past years. I even thought about going back to university. It's not too late, I can still make a career switch. But I can't think of anything that I want so badly that I'd go through all the trouble of being a poor student again at the age of thirty-five."

"Maybe you're just happy with your life." Hannah looked at her sideways.

"Yeah. I'm pretty happy, I suppose. The only thing

missing is..." Kristine hesitated.

"What?"

Kristine shook her head. "Never mind, it's stupid."

"Love?" Hannah asked, already knowing the answer.

Kristine nodded, her cheeks turning bright red.

"That's not stupid, Kristine. It's the one thing people want most in life. I can't deny that I've become a bit skeptical since Beth left me. But I still want to believe that I'll find love, when I'm ready."

"She hurt you badly, didn't she?" Kristine said, lowering her voice as she took Hannah's hand.

Hannah smiled, her body warming at the contact. "She did. But I'm also glad it's over. She wasn't the one for me, I know that now." She nodded towards the ice-hotel bus that would take the people who didn't want to go to church, back to their hotel. Gunnar, Sofia, Joshua, Sarah and Espen had got in. Werner and Charlotte were sitting in Dani's car, parked next to the bus. "Do you want to go back to the hotel?" she asked. "Or do you want to go to church?"

"I'm tempted to go to church," Kristine said. "I'm not really religious, but I can imagine that it's quite special here, even though the sermon will be in Norwegian and I won't understand a word of it."

"I'll come with you then." Hannah waved at Dani in the driver's seat and opened the back door to let Kristine in first. "I've never been to church before, so I'm actually quite curious."

"My God, I didn't expect this," Hannah said as she stared over a sea of light when they arrived. She felt a shiver down her spine as they entered the cemetery in front of the small, white wooden village church. It was lit up by hundreds of candles in deep, cylinder shaped candleholders, placed in front of the well-kept graves.

"It's beautiful," Kristine whispered, with reverence in her voice.

"People light candles on their family graves over Christmas," Dani explained. "To remember those who have passed." She nodded towards the queue in front of the church door. "Most people here aren't regular church goers but on Christmas Eve and Christmas Day, the church is always full. It's just as much a social affair as it is a religious gathering." She waved when someone called her name, then greeted other people she knew as they joined the queue.

After they had helped themselves to coffee and cake, provided by the local congregation, Dani guided them towards some free seats halfway down the row of benches. She scooted in first and immediately started chatting with the woman in front of her. Charlotte and Werner followed, whilst Hannah and Kristine sat down last, next to the aisle. The interior of the church was simple but beautifully handcrafted. Timber walls surrounded them and the elaborate hand-carved backrests on the timber benches carried the same pattern as the doors and the altar, the latter being situated underneath a big timber cross. A red carpet was laid out on the aisle and in front of the altar, where a chunky wooden lectern stood under the lights of an enormous crystal chandelier. Next to the altar was a woman wearing a black velvet dress who sat on a stool with a big golden harp between her knees. She was laughing and talking to the people in the front row. Everyone seemed to know each other here.

"I think you're going to like this," Dani whispered to them when the chattering died down and a sense of calm settled over the church. "I didn't elaborate too much on the sermon, because I didn't want people to think I was trying to drag them to church, but I promise you, you won't regret coming here tonight."

The lights were slowly dimmed until it was dark in the church, the only light coming from the candles on the altar. The harp player started playing softly, elegantly running her hands over the strings of her large instrument. A sound of sublime beauty spread through the church, drawing gasps from the audience. Kristine took hold of Hannah's hand as they waited in anticipation. Although Kristine wasn't a regular church-goer, she used to go every Sunday with her parents until she left home, just out of habit. But in Covington, harp music or candlelight had never been part of the sermon and their church certainly didn't look as charming as this one. A side door opened and youthful voices filled the church, softly at first, then louder as a girls' choir walked down the aisle, each holding a burning candle in their hands. They were dressed in long, black dresses and their hair hung loosely around their shoulders. Kristine shivered at the sight, the beautiful sound of their angelic voices bringing tears to her eyes. The atmosphere felt mystical, almost ritualistic. Hannah's hand squeezed hers when the choir reached the most perfect harmony and she knew Hannah felt touched by it too. For the next half hour, they were entranced by the performance, the next song even more beautiful than the previous. Sitting there, hand in hand, their eyes fixed on the choir, Kristine felt an energy between them, a connection that was way beyond a friendship or a crush. They communicated without speaking, sent each other signals through only a squeeze of a hand, or one knee pressed against the other. She felt ecstatically happy but also sad at the same time, as she reminded herself that what they had between them couldn't be forever.

# 11

## THE SNOW GLOBE

"Hey." Kristine smiled when Hannah opened her eyes. She'd been awake for hours, simply enjoying lying next to her, drinking her coffee.

"Hey," Hannah whispered, running a hand over Kristine's cheek. "What time is it?"

"Eight." Kristine didn't have to look at the clock, she could tell by the birdsong coming out of the speakers. In an hour, they would be louder, indicating that breakfast was ready.

"Why didn't you wake me up sooner?" Hannah pulled Kristine's naked body against hers. "I don't want to waste any more time than I need by sleeping."

"You were exhausted," Kristine said, rolling on top of her. She closed her eyes at the blissful feeling of Hannah's body tight against her own. They had returned to the hotel around eight last night but, by the time dinner was over, it was late. They had spent hours making love until they were both too tired to keep their eyes open. Kristine had slept for a little while but she kept waking up, wanting to look at Hannah, drink her in while she still could.

"I've run a bath." Kristine said in a soft voice, closing her eyes when Hannah's hand traced the inside of her thigh. "Care to join me?"

"Hmm..." Hannah raised her eyebrows with a mischievous smirk on her face. "Good thinking." She reluctantly removed her hand, waited for Kristine to get up and followed her into the bathroom, where steam was rising up from the long, wooden framed bath in front of the window. Seeing the candles Kristine had lined up on the windowsill of the dimly lit room brought a lump to her throat. "You're so sweet, Kristine," she whispered as she got in. Kristine sat down in between Hannah's legs and leaned back against her as she sank lower into the warm water. "Are you comfortable?"

"How could I not be?" Kristine leaned her head against Hannah's shoulder and moaned softly when Hannah took the rosemary scented bar of soap from the edge of the bath and started soaping her breasts first, then massaging them with both hands. Feeling the confident warm hands gliding over her skin, circling her breasts and caressing her nipples, aroused her immediately. Hannah's lips were next to Kristine's ear, her chin resting on her shoulder. Kristine could hear her breathing faster now and she knew Hannah was just as turned on as she was. One of Hannah's hands moved down, towards Kristine's belly, then slowly slipped between her thighs while the other stayed on her breasts, holding her tight as she laid back against her.

"Yes..." Kristine whispered. She gasped when Hannah's hand cupped her center, holding it there while she passionately kissed her neck and the very sensitive spot behind her ear. Kristine folded her arms around Hannah's neck, behind her, and turned her head sideways to look at her.

Hannah's lips pulled into a smile before they crashed

against Kristine's and parted, kissing her deeply. As they kissed her fingers began to move through Kristine's folds, making her grind into her hand, slow and sensual as the water splashed up against the sides of the bathtub. She loved the sensation of Kristine's body against her own in the warm water, Kristine's hungry mouth on hers, and the noises she made when she found her clit and rubbed her fingers against it, soft at first, then harder. Kristine trembled in her arms and whimpered but didn't break the kiss, not even when she began to tense up, her moans growing louder as Hannah circled her swollen flesh. Hannah knew she was close now and she brought her other hand down between Kristine's legs, entering her with two fingers. She wanted to feel her when she came.

"Yes..." Kristine gasped again as she pulled out of the kiss and looked up at Hannah with a look of sheer delight on her face. Then she bit her lower lip and closed her eyes, letting the orgasm wash over her, release flooding her features.

"Hey, Hannah, look at this," Kristine said as they left the bedroom to have breakfast. She picked up the red and white Christmas stocking, hanging on the door handle. "Oh, that's so sweet, there are farewell presents from Espen and Dani in here." She reached into the stocking and took out the two presents that were beautifully wrapped in white and gold striped wrapping paper with a gold ribbon tied around it.

"You must have been a good girl." Hannah said in a flirty tone as Kristine opened the first one.

"Oh my God, it's a block of that delicious goats' cheese." Kristine laughed. "Dani must have noticed me eating it for breakfast every morning. She's so thoughtful..." She opened the second present. "And a pair of hand-knitted socks. I love them," she said, holding up the navy socks with a white star-shaped pattern. Kristine pointed down the corridor to Hannah's room. "Looks like you've been a good girl too, Hannah."

Hannah walked over to her door and came back with her own stocking. She sighed with a big smile when she opened her first present, containing a pot of Dani's home-made blueberry jam with a red and white checked fabric covered top. The recipe was written on a label, stuck underneath. "She really is an angel." Hannah opened the other present and found the exact same pair of socks as Kristine's.

Kristine laughed. "We've spent two nights together and we've already got matching socks."

"It sure looks like it." Hannah put the jam and the socks back in her stocking and handed it to Kristine, with an amused look. "If someone had told me that before I came here, I would have laughed at them. You might as well drop these in your room, along with your own presents, since it looks like we've already moved in together," she joked. Then she fell silent for a moment, her smile widening. "Actually, I've just remembered. I got you a little going away present too, yesterday. From the gift shop at the ice-hotel. I passed it when I went to the toilet. I forgot to give it to you because you tend to distract me, Ms. Miller." Hannah winked playfully, then disappeared into her room coming back out with a paper bag. "Here. This is for you."

"For me?" Kristine's eyes widened as she reached into the bag and found a snow globe. Inside was a glass reindeer, surrounded by snowflakes.

"There's a switch underneath," Hannah said. "It produces green light, resembling the aurora. I thought you might like it."

Kristine started laughing as she shook the globe, surrounding the reindeer with shimmering white flakes.

"I'm sorry. Do you hate it?" Hannah asked, taken aback by Kristine's reaction. "I know it's a little tacky but..."

"No, no, it's not that," Kristine interrupted her. "I love it. It's just that..." She paused. "Wait, give me a second." She opened the door to her room and came out with the same bag that Hannah had just given her. "Merry Christmas," she said, handing the bag to Hannah. "I wasn't going to give it to you until tomorrow because I haven't had the chance to write the card yet."

"Hannah laughed as she opened the bag and saw the snow globe. "What? You got me the same one!"

"Great minds think alike." Kristine put her arms around Hannah and planted a tender kiss on her lips. Hannah kissed her back and pulled her into a tight embrace as she closed her eyes. They stood there for a few moments, holding each other.

"Thank you, Kristine." Hannah felt touched by the fact that Kristine had bought her a present. She rarely received presents from anyone apart from her best friend Mandy, who never forgot her birthday. In fact, she realized, it might be one of the few Christmas presents she'd ever been given. "I'll keep this behind the bar at my restaurant, so I can look at it whenever I want and remember you." Her words felt bittersweet as she said them out loud. Remembering Kristine somehow just wasn't good enough anymore.

Kristine stepped back, feeling a little melancholy herself. "And I'll keep mine next to my bed," she said in a soft voice. "So I'll never forget you."

## 12

## STARGAZING

"Are we almost there yet?" Kristine chuckled, realizing all too well that she sounded like a sulking child as she stopped to catch her breath. "I'm sorry, I need a moment."

"Look at you," Hannah said in a teasing tone. "You're over thirty years younger than Sofia and you can't even keep up with her." She pointed to Sofia, who was well ahead of them, walking in a brisk pace as if it was nothing.

"Yeah well, I'm pretty sure Gunnar let her sleep last night, so that gives her an advantage over me." Kristine looked up at the mountain. Each time she thought she was halfway, the peak seemed even further away. "Is it just me, or is this hill growing higher as we climb?"

Hannah laughed. "That would be you, I think. And you don't even have to drag this behind you." She held up the rope in her hand that was attached to a sled, big enough for two people. "Want me to pull you up to the top on this?"

"Of course not." Kristine straightened herself and started walking again. "But thank you for taking care of that. I feel bad that you're pulling it all the way up."

"Hey, I'm just trying to impress you," Hannah joked.

"I don't think you need to worry about impressing me anymore," Kristine said, catching up with her. She looped her arm through Hanna's as they continued their climb.

THEY WERE the last ones to arrive at the top, finally joining the rest of their group for a coffee as they sat on their sled, looking down at their own footprints in the snow.

"I didn't realize how steep it was until I got up here," Charlotte said, pulling her sled a little further from the edge as she grimaced. "But it sure is beautiful."

Kristine nodded, enthralled by the view. "It really is." Despite the dark, she could see everything clearly – from down the hill to the snow-covered lake, boats upside down on the shore and the hotel in the background, lit up by the spotlights outside the building. The edge of the woods ran along the right side of it, and around the back, creating a dense black wall of trees. Further away, to the left of the house, was the coastline and the lights of Kirkenes town, and above all that, were the stars.

"Do you guys see that really bright star up there?" Espen asked, pointing North. "That's Polaris, also known as the North Star."

"I've been seeing it a lot since I got here, Hannah said. "I was wondering if it was a satellite, it seems a lot closer than the other stars."

"Yes, it's certainly bright. It's also one of the most widely known stars." Espen explained, "It's located almost exactly above the North Pole, so people have been using it to navigate for centuries." He rummaged through his backpack and handed them a laminated sheet, each with constellations on them. "We're going to play a little game. Look at the images and see if you can spot these constellations. The ones on here are the ones most visible, even now, at three in the afternoon. Ursa Minor, which Polaris is part of, is the easiest to spot. Draco, Cassiopeia and Cepheus are all North too, and you know where the North is now." He smiled as excited murmurs and shrieks came from his guests when they started to recognize the shapes in the sky. Hannah and Kristine had fun trying to find them and, soon enough, Hannah started to notice other shapes as she looked around.

"What's that? The arrow shape," she asked Espen, pointing to a group of stars above them.

"Ah, the arrow. Well spotted." Espen shot her an impressed grin. "That's Orion. Or part of Orion." He opened his backpack again and handed out more laminated sheets. "This was actually part two of the quiz but, as you've already noticed a part of Orion, this is what it looks like."

Hannah looked at the image, then back up at the sky, mentally connecting the stars until she saw the belt, the torso and the limbs of a figure shooting an arrow.

"Yeah. I see it now." She took a picture with her phone. "Wow, this is fascinating. Can you see it, Kristine?"

Kristine's eyes narrowed as she kept looking from the image on her sheet to the sky and back. "Yes," she finally said, smiling. "And I can see Gemini too now, just above his head. Look. The figures are almost symmetrical." She pointed at the image of Gemini on her sheet as she pressed her cheek against Hannah's. They stayed there for a while, standing close together, stargazing and taking in the view as the sky turned darker and the stars shone even brighter.

"Everyone excited to go back down the easy way?" Espen yelled from his sled behind them. He laughed as his guests anxiously looked over the edge, their sleds at least ten feet apart.

"I'm not so sure," Werner said. "This seems more like the dangerous way than the easy way if you ask me."

"If you're uncomfortable, you can walk down, of course," Espen continued. "But there's a brake and you'll be able to steer it so it's not like you'll be throwing yourself into the deep without any control. I personally recommend just going for it, straight ahead, as fast as you can. These sleds are very sturdy, and I promise you, they're not going to tip over. The faster you go, the further you'll go, and that means less walking."

"Less walking sounds good," Kristine said behind Hannah, who was sitting at the front of the sled, between her legs. Her arms were wrapped tight around Hannah's waist, finally making Hannah's fantasy come true.

"Are you sure?" Hannah turned around and shot her a challenging look. The steepness was making her a little nervous but if Kristine was comfortable with it, then she wasn't going to hold back. Besides, she didn't think Espen would let them do this if it was dangerous.

"I'm sure. No more walking for me today." Kristine tightened her grip around Hannah.

"Okay then." Hannah nodded to Espen, letting him know that they were ready. He walked over to them, checked that their legs were secure, and pushed their sled over the edge. They picked up speed within seconds, and both Hannah and Kristine screamed as they zoomed down the mountain, straight ahead towards the lake. It took all of Hannah's willpower not to use the brake as they went faster and faster until they finally reached the flat surface of the lake. As they continued to glide, they heard more screams behind them from other people making their way down.

“This is great,” Kristine yelled. “We’re already halfway across the lake and we’ve only just started to slow down. Keep going.”

“I can’t control it, can I?” Hannah yelled back at her, laughing. Their sled came to a halt only about twenty yards from the shore.

“Oh God, that was fun.” Kristine was still grinning from ear to ear when Hannah got off the sled and straightened herself on shaky legs.

“It was but I’m also glad it’s over.” She laughed again as she took hold of the rope and started pulling the sled with Kristine still on it, back to the hotel.

## 13

## STORIES AROUND THE CAMPFIRE

"I feel sad that it's our last night together." Kristine's voice was soft when she spoke. She looked up at Hannah from the book she was reading, curled up on the couch next to the fireplace. They'd been warming up after their sledging adventure, both laying out on each end of the big sofa while the rest of the group were outside, in the sauna, or taking a nap. Every now and then, Kristine would stretch her long, lithe limbs, and Hannah would take her foot in her hand and massage it, desperately needing the contact.

"Yeah." Hannah gave her a sad smile. Their whirlwind holiday romance was coming to an end and it stung to know that she might never see Kristine again. Long distance relationships rarely worked in her opinion and, even if they wanted to try, she could never get away from the restaurant for longer than a week. She was just too far away. Besides, Hannah wasn't in the right place to jump into a relationship, especially not one that would be this complicated, with Kristine, whom she was only just getting to know, living in a different time zone, and herself working sixteen hours a day. "I wish we had more time..." She fell silent for a moment. "But then again, if we did have more time, it would only be harder to say goodbye. This way, it is what it is, right? Wonderful nights and beautiful memories. I'll never forget you, Kristine. I'll never forget *this*. I want you to know that."

"I'll never forget you either." Kristine put her book down and shuffled a little closer. "How could I?" She smiled. "I don't know if it's this place, the magic of the northern lights, the Christmas spirit here, or the fact that you're simply irresistible... but this week has been magical. I'll always cherish it."

Hannah put her book down too. "Will you spend the night with me again?"

"Of course. You don't have to ask me that." Kristine grinned. "I thought that was a given. There's no way I'm going to be apart from you on our last night..."

"Good." Hannah turned in her seat, facing Kristine. "Because I've got plans for you." Her eyes darkened as they locked with Kristine's.

"You have no idea what you do to me when you look at me like that," Kristine said, lowering her voice. "It turns me on so badly." She licked her lips unconsciously while she twirled a lock of hair around her finger.

Hannah shot her a flirty look. "Oh yeah?" She reached out for Kristine's waist, tracing her fingers over her curvy hip. "And I like you in these leggings. Your ass is a delight to look at. Of course I prefer them off..." she smiled. "But for now, this is pretty great." She looked over her shoulder as Dani approached them with a bowl of pickled cabbage that she was about to take outside.

"I'm serving dinner," she told them. "But if you two prefer to be alone, I can take it to you room later, it's not a..."

"No, no, of course not." Kristine interrupted her. She stood up from the sofa.

"Absolutely not." Hannah followed suit. "We just need to put on our snowsuits and then we'll come and help you with the food." She smiled at Dani. "Thank you again for the gifts by the way. That was really sweet. And I'd love to get something for you and Espen as a thank you for your wonderful hospitality but it's a little hard without a shopping mall around the corner..."

"Oh, don't be silly," Dani interrupted her. "It's just a little something. We always give out gifts, but we like to wait a couple of days, so we get to know our guests a little. Apart from the socks." She laughed. "Everyone gets socks." She put the bowl on the edge of the couch and sat down next to it. "We're closed for three months a year. Six weeks in spring and six weeks in autumn. It's not like there's much else to do around here other than knit. The Wi-Fi connection isn't even good enough to stream a movie and we go on a nice summer vacation each year, but that's still only two weeks. So, I knit socks because they're the only thing I know how to make. And Christmas is the perfect opportunity to give them out."

"Well, as a thank you for being so lovely, I just want you to know that my menu next month will have a new brunch dish on it," Hannah said. "It's called 'Dani Christensen's buttermilk waffles with blueberry jam' – everyone in London will be raving about it."

"Really?" Dani seemed genuinely excited about that prospect.

"I promise." Hannah winked. "I'll send you the link to my website."

. . .

"The trolls..." Espen said, holding a flashlight under his chin as he pulled his face into a creepy grimace, "They're no joke." He'd been telling stories from Norse mythology and Scandinavian folklore over dinner. Espen was a good storyteller and his guests had been hanging on his every word. "They were initially just stories made up to scare children, to stop them from wandering too far into the woods," he said. "But in the end, we ended up scaring ourselves." He laughed. "I know trolls don't really exist but on a dark winter's night, I think twice before I wander out there by myself," he continued, pointing at the dense patch of woods where Hannah and Kristine had found their Christmas tree. "If I hear rustling behind me, my first thought isn't that it's an elk, or a bear. Because late at night, when the light turns that mystical blue, and the silence falls like a blanket over the world, the chance of trolls and huldras existing will always cross my mind, even if it's just for a split second."

"What's a huldra?" Charlotte asked.

"The huldra comes from Swedish mythology. It's a beautiful, flirtatious young woman with long hair who lives in the woods but she has a cow's tail that she hides behind her back when she encounters people. She's from the underworld, a lost soul, and she seduces people to be with her, taking them to her dark place."

"And then there's 'the mare'," Dani added. "She's a female vette, a species of mythical creatures that live close to humans. She sits beside you on your bed while you sleep and feeds off the nightmares she gives you. That's where 'mareritt', the Norwegian word for nightmare, comes from."

"Are there any handsome males in Norwegian mythology?" Sofia asked with a chuckle. She looked towards the woods, suddenly feeling a little less comfortable. "Or are they all female?"

"No, they're not all female, there are many male mythical creatures too." Dani looked around the group. "You've all heard about the 'nisser', of course, the Christmas creatures that people decorate their homes with this time of year. They're friendly pranksters, usually up to no good. They live in the barn and over Christmas they fulfil the same function as Santa does in most countries. Besides nisser, trolls are also male, and elves can be male too. None of them are attractive though, apart from Fossegrimmen. He is a handsome young man who plays the fiddle." She laughed and turned to Sofia. "Naked under a waterfall, if I may add. He plays the music of nature in its purest form. When fiddle players are extremely talented, it is said that they've sold their soul in exchange for his skills because he played like a god."

"Speaking of gods... There she is again." Gunnar stood up and pointed towards a faint light that was starting to appear in front of them over the mountains. Kristine thought that the word *she*, seemed appropriate. For if Aurora really was a goddess, Kristine was sure her nearness was having some kind of effect on Hannah tonight because wow... she sure seemed inspired. She'd been giving her looks in front of everyone and wasn't holding back with her tactile and flirty ways. Kristine felt special and wanted, and it was good to feel that way, because it had been too long since she'd been the object of someone's desire. Hannah was the sexiest woman she'd ever met and she was perfect for her in every single way. Her smile, her laugh, her energy, her body, the way she made Kristine feel and the way she touched her and looked at her when they made love, with a look of pure lust and fascination. Kristine was so turned on by now that she physically ached to be touched each time their eyes locked.

"Can I just say, that I had a really good time with every single one of you and I've really enjoyed getting to know you all." Hannah surprised herself by the words that'd just come out of her mouth unplanned but she meant it. For a week, they'd felt like a little family, sharing stories, jokes and even secrets. Eight strangers, ten including Espen and Dani, with very little in common. It had been wonderful. Like Dani had told her, the effect of the dark had made them open up to each other and seeing the wonders of the aurora together had bonded them somehow.

"So have I." Sofia gave her a sweet smile. "It's been amazing and the thought that I won't see you guys again makes me a little sad right now."

"Me too," Sarah chipped in. "Is this normal?" She asked Dani. "I mean, do you ever have people who fight, or people who can't stand each other?"

"Not really." Dani smiled. "It's pretty consistent and that's what I love about this job. People always leave happy, with fond memories and new friendships. The most important lesson I've learned after starting these group holidays, is that friends don't always have to be close. You can keep them in your heart and in your thoughts. You don't have to make promises to see each other again. If it happens, it happens and if it doesn't ..." She made sure not to look in Kristine and Hannah's direction. "Well, then you'll always have the memories, and the best memories never fade."

Hannah looked down at her lap, Kristine's hand resting in hers on her thigh. Dani's words stung. She felt Kristine's hand tighten as they entwined their fingers and she didn't want to let go ever again. What were the odds of meeting someone she felt such a deep connection with, coupled with a mutual attraction so strong, that it was impossible to ignore? And more than that, what were the odds of meeting someone like Kristine here, amongst a small group of strangers, at the end of the world? But then again, what were the odds she'd ever see her again? They were parting ways tomorrow. Kristine would continue her Scandinavian adventure and Hannah would go straight to work, throwing herself back into her hectic London life. She'd told herself many times over the past days not to be so dramatic. For a moment, she'd even considered that she might be losing it, that the dark had made her go crazy somehow, making her crush unnaturally on someone she'd only just met. But both the pain and the joy felt very real. Gasps from the others around her made her turn her eyes back to the sky, it was turning green now, as a beautiful glow spread out over them. Feeling no less captivated than she had the first time she'd seen the phenomenon, she sank deeper into her chair and relaxed as they watched the show.

"Do you want to come to my room, or shall I come to yours?" Kristine asked when they'd reached the landing. "Or would you prefer to be alone tonight?"

"Yours?" Hannah smiled, letting her eyes linger on Kristine's. Of course she wanted to spend the night with Kristine. It was all she'd been thinking of for the past hours. The last two nights had been a revelation, a mind-blowing experience. Their bodies fit so perfectly together and they were completely attuned to each other's needs and desires. Hannah hadn't known this kind of passion even existed and she was pretty sure from Kristine's reaction on their first night, that she was just as surprised at how their initial attraction to each other had resulted in a gravitation so enormous, and so delightful, that neither of them would be able to resist each other, even if they tried.

"I need to have a quick shower, I've been sweating in front of the fire. I'll be ten minutes." Hannah said.

"Hurry up," Kristine replied, her eyes full of longing as they shifted to Hannah's lips.

A LITTLE LATER, there was a short knock on Kristine's door, and her breath caught when

she opened it, unprepared for the effect Hannah with wet hair would have on her. Her hair was combed back, making her attractive face and her dark brown eyes stand out even more. Hannah's robe was loosely tied around her waist, her skin still damp - as if she had run over in a hurry.

"Hey..." Hannah stepped into the room and swiftly locked the door behind her before glancing at Kristine. Kristine was wearing the same hotel robe, with an enticing cleavage on display.

"Hi.'

They stood there for a couple of electrifying seconds, the pull between them so strong that it was almost visible. Hannah smiled and stepped towards Kristine and gave her a soft kiss on her cheek before pressing her mouth against her ear.

"At least we won't have to bother with five layers of clothing tonight," she whispered. Kristine shivered when she felt Hannah's breath against her ear and her hands sneaking under her robe, cupping her ass. Hannah let her lips linger on Kristine's ear, then traced her jaw with her mouth before bringing it back to her earlobe, biting it gently. "You drive me wild, Kristine." She squeezed Kristine's ass before she ran her hands up towards her waist and around her back, hiking up her robe. Kristine closed her eyes at the words, leaning back against the wall when her legs became unsteady. Hannah tilted her head, her mouth close to Kristine's now. She could feel her ragged breathing, a hint of mint on her breath. She liked playing this game, always had. Teasing, dragging out the moment until she'd let herself go, giving Kristine everything she wanted and more. She felt more confident as the days had passed and she could tell Kristine felt comfortable around her too. A smile played around her lips when Kristine opened her blue eyes to meet Hannah's stare. Her eyes were hazy, lustful. She leaned in to kiss Hannah, but Hannah moved back, her grin widening.

"Are you trying to kill me?" Kristine whispered with a chuckle. "Kiss me already."

Hannah shook her head as she moved her mouth closer to Kristine's again. "Patience darling." She dug her nails into Kristine's skin and traced them down her back before reaching her hips, keeping their eyes locked. It was beautiful, watching Kristine shiver at her touch. She loved the way Kristine's eyelashes fluttered, how her lips parted when she was aroused, those full lips so luscious and inviting. Without warning, she crashed her mouth into Kristine's and pressed herself against her as she kissed her deeply. A whimper escaped Kristine's mouth and she reached out to lace her fingers through Hannah's hair, pulling her in closer. Hannah was unable to hold back at the sound of her pleasure. She moved a hand around Kristine's hips to the front and slipped it between her legs, cupping her center hard before slowly tracing her fingers upwards.

"Fuck!" Kristine cried out as her legs almost gave way underneath her.

Hannah pulled away to watch her whimper. "Did you like that?" She didn't wait for an answer as she repeated the movement, burying her fingers deeper between Kristine's folds this time. Hannah felt her wetness against her hand and bit her lip when a warm tingle spread between her legs. Just touching Kristine did that to her. Kristine moaned louder, her hands still in Hannah's hair.

"Uhuh," she muttered, steadying herself against the wall as she ground her hips against Hannah's hand.

"More?" Hannah asked, lifting Kristine's chin to face her. Kristine looked at her through eyes that were oozing desire. Again, Hannah didn't wait for an answer. She moved her hand back down and slipped two fingers inside Kristine's warm wetness, causing her to gasp in pleasure. She held her fingers there for a moment, then penetrated her deeper, watching Kristine's expression turn darker and her chest heave as her breathing became more erratic. It was turning Hannah on like nothing else, knowing she could make her feel this way. Kristine's hips met her rhythm as she moved in and out of her, harder and faster now, using her other hand to pull Kristine's robe off her shoulders until it fell down on the floor. Her eyes shifted to Kristine's full breasts and her sensual naked body that was all hers now, and her mouth was drawn to her breasts as if she had no control over her actions. She circled her tongue around a hard nipple and closed her lips around it, tasting her flesh.

"Oh God. Yes, Hannah." Kristine threw her head back against the wall as her body stiffened before she started shaking uncontrollably. Hannah straightened herself again, her eyes fixated on Kristine's face as she climaxed, tiny drops of sweat pearling on her forehead. She felt Kristine contracting around her fingers, her limbs trembling, and finally she watched as she closed her eyes in delight. She looked free and ecstatic and so incredibly beautiful. Hannah held Kristine up when she started to relax, still inside her as she stroked her hair.

Kristine let out a deep sigh and opened her eyes again. "God, Hannah. You really know how to drive a girl crazy. That was..." she shook her head, took a deep breath and exhaled. "Never mind. I'm speechless." Hannah tried really hard not to pull a smug grin but it was hard with Kristine looking like she'd just had the best sex of her life. Kristine whimpered again when she slowly pulled out of her.

"I think you might very well be the sexiest woman alive," was all she could manage to say.

"I think that's debatable," Kristine replied, removing the belt on Hannah's robe. She took off the robe and stared at Hannah's body, unconsciously licking her lips. "Because you look pretty sexy to me too." She reached out to touch Hannah's breasts and leaned in for a smoldering kiss, guiding Hannah towards the bed. Hannah let herself fall down when they'd reached the end of the bed, moving backwards as Kristine followed her, crawling towards her on her hands and knees.

"Now it's my turn," she said, her voice hoarse. She pushed Hannah down into the pillows with a hand on her chest and straddled her hips.

Hannah looked up at Kristine's piercing blue eyes, her soft tanned skin, the curve of her hips and her breasts that looked too good not to touch. She reached out for them but Kristine took her hands and pinned then down above her head on the pillow.

"I can play that game too, you know," Kristine whispered. She gave Hannah a mischievous smile as she bent forward, her mouth hovering over Hannah's lips. Hannah instinctively lifted her head, longing for Kristine's mouth.

"Kiss me," she said.

"Nah-ah." Kristine moved away a little, equally teasing her. She was clearly having fun. Slowly, she traced a finger over Hannah's neck and her breasts, down to her bellybutton, where she let it rest between her own legs. She let her eyes roam over Hannah as if studying every inch of her, taking in her dark eyes, her sharp jawline, her shoulders and her arms that were toned from years in hospitality, her small but beautiful breasts, the tattoo of a bird on her ribcage, underneath her left breast, the beauty mark on her stomach, almost resembling a heart, and her tight abs. "I like looking at you," she whispered, before moving back to place a kiss on the beauty mark.

Hannah shivered at the warm lips on her stomach and Kristine's hair that tickled her between her legs. She'd never seen anyone look at her like that, not even Beth. She closed her eyes when Kristine's mouth moved down towards her hips, then kissed the inside of her thigh as she spread her legs apart. The way Kristine took her time, exploring every part of her almost drove her crazy with anticipation and, by the time Kristine's tongue had roamed over her center, she could barely contain her muffled cries, the sound dampened by her hand over her mouth. Kristine looked up at her for a moment and smiled before she sank deeper into Hannah, plunging her tongue inside her. Hannah quivered, lifting her hips to meet Kristine's warm mouth. The touch of Kristine's tongue felt like magic while her hands roamed over her thighs and her stomach, then further down again, caressing the patch of dark hair between Hannah's legs before she circled her clit with the palm of her hand. Hannah moaned louder as her orgasm took over with surprising force.

"Yes, Kristine... Yes!" Kristine savored the moment as Hannah's thighs clamped around her head as she tasted her, as she felt her legs trembling, heard the noises she was making, and as she panted out a string of post-orgasmic breaths. Hannah's hand was in hers now, their fingers entwined. She wanted to remember everything about this moment. When Hannah's breathing finally calmed down, she slowly kissed her way back up, meeting her lips. Hannah wrapped her arms around Kristine as they kissed, slow and deep, not nearly close to being finished with her.

## 14

## REFLECTIONS

"Ready to leave?" Hannah asked. She sat down next to Kristine outside, where the campfire was blazing, and handed her a mug of coffee. It was eleven in the morning and the faint twilight was causing the sky to slowly shift from black to a deep, dark blue. The stars were still visible, and there were so many – some clustered together, and some brighter than others. Kristine wasn't wearing her snowsuit today. Just a pair of jeans, a white cable-knit sweater over her base layers, and a hand-knitted navy scarf that matched her gloves. Her blonde hair was tucked into the scarf that also covered the lower half of her face. She'd gotten dressed while Hannah had a shower in her own room and packed up her clothes, of which she'd only worn about a third.

"Not really." Kristine yawned and stretched her arms out above her head before gratefully accepting the coffee. "I'm not even packed yet. I just wanted to enjoy this view for a little longer before I go. I'm going to miss it." Her gaze roamed over the snow-covered lake before she turned to

Hannah with a look in her eyes that caused a lump to settle in Hannah's throat. "But I'm going to miss you the most," she added. "It's been..." she fell silent for a moment. "Well, I'm not going to lie, it's been incredibly special to me."

Hannah was touched by her honesty. "It's been special to me too," she said. "If it were under any other circumstances, I'd ask you out on a date but since we live on different continents..." She wanted nothing more than to ask Kristine to prolong her holiday, and visit her in London, but she was afraid that might be too much to ask after their brief four-day romance.

"Yeah." Kristine sighed. "We could stay in contact?" she tried carefully. "No strings of course," she hastily added. "Just an email every now and then, or a phone call?"

Hannah's heart warmed at Kristine's words. At least she'd had the courage to bring up the possibility, unlike herself.

"I'd love that," she said, not bothering to hide how keen she was at the prospect of staying in touch. "We could Skype?' She smiled. "And of course, no strings. I won't expect anything from you but it would be a shame to never speak to each other again, right?"

Kristine now had a big grin on her face. "Really? You wouldn't mind?" She leaned over the plastic armrest of her chair and gave Hannah a soft kiss on her cheek. "Thank you. That makes it a little easier to leave today."

"Yeah." Hannah grimaced. "Or maybe not." She got out of her chair, bent over Kristine and kissed her. The kiss was both tender and electrifying as they sank into each other's warmth in the dark by the fire. Hannah smiled and straightened herself when they got to that point once again, that moment where they seemed unable to stop. "Want me to help you with anything?" She asked.

"I still have an hour, so I'll be fine," Kristine said, standing up too. "You'll only distract me with your kisses and I'll probably end up missing my flight." She paused. "What time is your flight?"

"Not until four." Hannah took her hand as they walked back to the hotel together. "We're all on the same one to Oslo, we then take our separate connections. Charlotte and Werner are flying to Frankfurt tonight, Sarah and Josh are going to Paris tomorrow and I've got a very tight connection to London."

"At least you'll have some company on the first part of your journey."

"I'm not sure I'll be in the mood for company," Hannah said. She cursed herself for being so dramatic but she just couldn't help herself. Instead she decided to change the subject. "So, are you looking forward to going to Copenhagen?"

Kristine shrugged. "Yes, I am, I suppose. I'm excited to see the city, for sure. And Sofia and Gunnar have invited me over to spend New Year's Eve with them, which was very kind. They live by the harbor and apparently they get incredible views of the fireworks from their balcony. But it's bittersweet. I know I sound silly saying this but I'll probably be missing you most of the time." She forced a smile, trying to pull herself together. "Are you looking forward to going back to London?"

"Not really." Hannah let out a chuckle. "I've been ignoring my phone all week, so I have no idea what mess I'll be returning to. I trust my staff of course, and I'm sure they will have kept everything under control to the best of their abilities, but everything seems so insignificant now, after this week. This might sound strange but I feel like I've been away for much longer than I really have and I'm not ready to settle back into normal life yet. You know, work, friends, the simple concept of day and night… It's like I need the time to process everything first. I've thought about things here that I never, ever, think about, like where I came from and why I am the way I am. They were only fleeting thoughts, barely scraping the surface, but they stuck, somehow." Hannah arched an eyebrow as she turned to Kristine. "I'm sorry, I'm being a bit deep here, and this is usually not me, I promise." She'd shocked herself once again by being so honest. Her roots were something she'd decided a long time ago, were not important. It'd never mattered to her who her birth-mother was. She had ruined her youth and that was enough to block her out of Hannah's mind forever. But the northern lights had seeped into her soul, forced her to think about things bigger than herself, and with that came questions.

"Are you thinking of looking into your birth records?" Kristine asked carefully, as if reading her mind.

"Yeah. I'm thinking about it." Hannah sighed. "And the fact that I'm thinking about it, whether I'll do it or not, is a big thing for me."

"I understand." Kristine stopped when they were in front of the door. "Well, if you ever want to talk about it, I'm only a phone call away."

"Thank you." Hannah hesitated. "You know, I've never told anyone I was adopted. The only person who knows is my best friend, Mandy. I don't tend to talk to people the way I talk to you."

"Was that because it seemed easier to talk to someone you thought you'd never see again?"

"Maybe, at first, yeah." Hannah confessed.

Kristine winked as she opened the door for Hannah. "Well, you're not going to get rid of me that easily, so brace yourself for midnight Skype calls and tons of text messages. I'm going to write down my details for you and you need to give me yours." On that positive note they stepped back into the hotel.

## 15

## A PROMISE

"I'm ready if you are," Dani said, giving Kristine's arm a squeeze as she walked past her to grab her coat in the hallway. Kristine's suitcase and duffel bag were already stacked up by the door. She'd said goodbye to everyone and she was ready to go.

"Sure. I just need a minute." Kristine waved from the doorway at Hannah, who was pretending to read her book on the sofa, determined not to show how sad she really was after their last kiss in Kristine's room. She jumped up when Kristine called her over, threw her book on the sofa and walked into the hallway.

"What's up? Did you forget something?"

"No, I was just thinking..." Kristine said, casting a quick glance at Dani, who was still by the front door. "Well, I was thinking that maybe..."

Dani sensed Kristine's need for privacy and quickly zipped up her coat. "I'm going to warm up the car," she said. "Take you time."

"What were you thinking?" Hannah asked after Dani had closed the door behind her. Kristine's cheeks turned red and she shuffled on the spot. It was endearing to watch and Hannah felt an urge to put her arms around her. But she wanted to hear what Kristine had to say first, because the uncertain look in her eyes was giving her a spark of hope. Hope of what, she wasn't sure, but she had the feeling that whatever Kristine had to say, would make her feel a little better.

"I can take two weeks off in March," Kristine blurted out. "I always take a two week vacation in March..." She nervously looked down at her feet. "I've never been to London, and I was wondering if you'd want to see me if I decide to go there. I'll book a hotel, of course. You won't have to put me up but I'd really like to hang out with you." It had been a spur-of-the-moment thought, just an idea as she was putting on her coat. But she had to ask, because the idea of never seeing Hannah again just wasn't an option.

Hannah's heart almost burst at the words. "Would you really do that? Would you really come to London?" Only a day ago, the idea had dawned on her too, although discussing it had seemed crazy. But now that Kristine was leaving, it was as if everything had suddenly fallen into place and everything was going to be okay. She really wanted to see Kristine too. Not only did she want it, she needed it with every fiber of her being.

"If you want me to." Kristine anxiously bit her lip, holding her breath for Hannah to reply.

"Are you crazy? I'd love to see you in March." Hannah was beaming now, not even attempting to contain her excitement. "But forget about the hotel. You have to stay with me..." She grinned. "In my bed, I insist."

Kristine smiled and flung her arms around her neck. "Oh my God, Hannah. You have no idea how happy you've made me just by saying that." She stepped away and locked her eyes with Hannah's, taking her in one last time. "Are you sure?"

"Of course I'm sure." Hannah leaned in and kissed Kristine, pulling her hard against her as they both sank into a kiss that was so intense, so all-consuming, that they lost themselves right there, in the hallway, with the door to the living room wide open. The sound of shuffling footsteps broke them up and Hannah stepped back, still with a wide grin on her face. The sound of Gunnar walking on his slippers was unique, the way he dragged his feet across the floor in a lazy manner. They could hear his pace accelerating and they both laughed, knowing he'd caught them once again.

"I'll see you in March then," Hannah whispered, her forehead pressed against Kristine's. "Please promise me you'll come, I'll be counting down the days."

Kristine gave her another fleeting kiss before she picked up her bags and opened the door.

"I promise. I'll see you in March."

**To be continued in 'Southern Roots'....**

**Coming in 2019**

# THE SEVEN COOKIES OF CHRISTMAS

A NORWEGIAN TRADITION

Who doesn't like a bit of baking over Christmas? I certainly do, and I thought it might be fun to include some of my mother's Norwegian cookie recipes, so you can join in with Hannah & Kristine and give it a go yourself. I've substituted two kinds of cookies that appear in Northern Lights with other recipes that are also popular Christmas cookies in Norway, as I am assuming no one outside Scandinavia will have the special irons required to make these. Therefore you should only need standard kitchen equipment, and you can even substitute a rolling pin for a wine bottle—it works just fine. I've personally tested all the recipes to see if they could be made without an electric mixer, and although I couldn't lift my right arm the next day, the cookies tasted great! With *tsp*, I mean a regular teaspoon you stir your coffee with, and with *tbsp*, I mean a regular spoon you eat soup with, so if it doesn't fit in your mouth, it's too big... One final note – please be aware that these recipes make big batches, they are made to be shared & are often given as gifts to friends & family at Christmas.

Happy baking and have a fabulous Christmas!

Lise

## PEPPERKAKER

MAKES ABOUT 40 SMALL COOKIES

Ingredients

- 2 eggs
- 125 gr sugar / 0.6 cup / 4.4 oz
- 50 ml full fat cream / 0.2 cup
- 100 ml sour cream / 0.4 cup
- 390 gr white flour / 2.4 cups / 10.2 oz
- 3 tsp baking powder
- ½ tsp cardamom
- Sugar and icing sugar to decorate
- Vegetable oil to deep-fry

1. Cream the butter until light and fluffy, then beat in the sugar (this can be done by hand or using a mixer).

2. Add in the spices, the golden syrup, then the flour and continue to mix until everything is blended well.

3. Leave the dough to cool in the fridge for 2 hours.

4. After cooling, roll out the dough and use a cookie cutter

to cut out shapes. I like to use Christmas tree shapes for this recipe. If you don't have cookie cutters, you can simply roll the dough into a sausage shape and slice off rounds.

5. Line your baking sheet(s) with parchment paper and bake the cookies in a pre-heated oven for 10 minutes, 180 C / 360 F / GM 4.

6. After removing from the oven leave the cookies to cool down and firm up. Easy!

## SMULTRINGER

MAKES ABOUT 40-50 SMALL DOUGHNUTS

Ingredients

- 2 eggs
- 125 gr sugar / 0.6 cup / 4.4 oz
- 50 ml full fat cream / 0.2 cup
- 100 ml sour cream / 0.4 cup
- 390 gr white flour / 2.4 cups / 10.2 oz
- 3 tsp baking powder
- ½ tsp cardamom
- Sugar and icing sugar to decorate
- Vegetable oil to deep-fry

1. Beat the eggs and sugar together until the mixture starts to stiffen (this can be done by hand or using a mixer).

2. Add in the cream and the sour cream, then add the flour, the baking powder and finally the cardamom.

3. Mix again until all is blended well. The dough should look a little stringy at this stage.

4. Leave the dough to cool in the fridge for half an hour.

5. Flour your work surface, your hands and your rolling pin and roll out the dough to a 1cm thickness. Use basic round cookie cutters of two different sizes, or an espresso cup to create the outer edge, and a small bottle top to cut out the inner part. After you've created your shapes, simply tear away the dough in between the circles and the inner parts of the doughnuts and use the scraps to make another batch.

6. Heat up frying oil in a big pan (or set your deep fat fryer to 165 C / 330F). When the oil has reached temperature place the smultringer in the oil. They will float to the top so don't put too many in the pan/fryer at the same time. Turn them after a while so they're a nice golden brown on both sides (not too dark or they will be dry), then put them on a paper towel to drain most of the excess fat off.

7. To finish, mix icing sugar and sugar together in a bowl and coat the smultringer on both sides while they're still hot, then lay them on a cold plate to cool.

## BERLINERKRANSER

MAKES ABOUT 30 COOKIES

Ingredients

2 hard-boiled egg yolks
2 raw egg yolks
200 gr sugar / 1 cup / 7 oz
320 gr white flour / 2 ½ cup / 11.2 oz
225 gr butter / 1 cup / 8 oz
1 ½ tsp vanilla sugar
Pearl sugar to decorate

1. Cut the butter into small chunks and leave them out of the fridge to soften.

2. Mix the cooked and raw egg yolks together in a bowl until you get a smooth mixture. Set the raw egg white aside for later.

3. Mix in the sugar and vanilla sugar and then combine the flour and the butter, adding alternatively until the mixture resembles a soft dough. You can do this by hand, which will give you a rigorous work-out, or with a mixer.

4. Leave the mixture to cool in the fridge for at least an hour.

5. Pre-heat the oven to 175 C / 350 F / GM 4.

6. Take chunks off the dough and roll into thin sausage shapes of around 12 cm long, about the thickness of your fingers. Now, create a wreath shape by folding one end over the other, letting them cross, this should leave a small hole in the middle.

7. Brush the cookies with egg white and decorate by sprinkling them with pearl sugar.

8. To finish, place the cookies on a parchment lined baking sheet, making sure to leave some space between them as they will expand in the oven. Bake them for about 15 minutes, then let then cool down. They will become harder as they cool and your kitchen will fill with the scent of vanilla!

## SANDKAKER

MAKES ABOUT 30

Ingredients

225 gr butter / 1 cup / 8 oz
255 gr white flour / 1.8 cup / 8 oz
130 gr ground almonds / 1 1/8 cup / 4.6 oz
1 egg
100 gr sugar / ½ cup / 3 ½ oz
For the filling:
200 ml full fat cream / 0.8 cup
200 ml sour cream / 0.8 cup
Berries of your choice
You will also need tartlet or muffin tins to make these.

1. Rub cubed butter into the flour until you're left with a mixture that resembles fine breadcrumbs.

2. Mix in the ground almonds, the sugar and the egg to the mixture. The mixture should now be forming small clumps and have a sand-like texture to it. Leave the dough to cool in the fridge for an hour.

3. Pre-heat your oven to 175 C / 350 F / GM 4.

4. After you have removed the dough from the fridge, press it firmly into the tartlet tins before then placing them onto a baking sheet. Bake them for about 13 minutes, or until they are slightly brown around the edges. Let them cool down completely before you even attempt to remove the cookies from the tins.

5. Mix the cream and sour cream and place a dollop into each sandkake, then, top them up with berries of your choice. Yum!

## SIRUPSNIPPERS

MAKES AROUND 50 COOKIES

Ingredients

150 ml cream / 0.6 cup
150 ml golden syrup / 0.6 cup
150 gr sugar / 0.6 cup / 5.2 oz
100 gr butter / 0.4 cup / 3.5 oz
450 gr white flour / 3.6 cup / 15.9 oz
¼ tsp ground star anise
¼ tsp ground black pepper
¼ tsp ground cinnamon
¼ tsp ground ginger
¾ tsp baking powder
¾ tsp baking soda
1 egg white to glaze
Almonds, blanched, for decorating

1. Melt the butter in a pan.

2. In another pan bring the cream, syrup and sugar to a boil and then add in the melted butter before removing from the heat.

3. Whisk in the dry ingredients and kneed into a dough. Leave the dough in the fridge overnight.

4. The next morning, remove the dough from the fridge - it should be quite tough in appearance at this stage.

5. Preheat the oven to 175 C / 350 F / GM4, and flour the worksurface, your hands and the rolling pin.

6. Roll out the dough until very thin, turn it around, and repeat until the dough is almost transparent. It might appear too thin or too flimsy for a cookie, but this is correct. Cut out into diamond shapes, place them on a parchment lined baking sheet and push half an almond into the middle of each cookie. Glaze them with egg white and bake for 5-7 minutes or until golden brown. Place on a plate to cool down. They will make your kitchen smell really Christmassy!

## FATTIGMAN

MAKES ABOUT 35 COOKIES

Ingredients

- 4 egg yolks
- 2 whole eggs
- 7 tbsp of sugar
- 120 ml cream / ½ cup
- 385 gr white flour / 3 cups / 13 ½ oz
- 1 ½ tbsp brandy
- A pinch of salt
- ½ tsp vanilla essence
- 1 tsp ground cardamom
- Vegetable oil or sunflower oil to deep-fry
- Icing sugar to decorate

1. Mix the eggs with the brandy and have a shot while you're at it!

2. Add the vanilla, cardamom, salt and cream, then fold in the flour. Do this by hand, preferably with a wooden spoon. It should not be beaten, just folded and blended gently until

it's all mixed together. Add a little extra flour to the mixture if it's still a little too sticky to roll out.

3. Dust your work surface, your hands and your rolling pin with flour and roll the dough out thin. Cut out diamond shapes and make a small cut in the middle of each diamond. Fold one end of the diamond through the hole in the center and pull it out on the other side. You now have a 'bow' (ish) shape. Don't worry if they don't look pretty, they'll puff up when you deep-fry them.

4. Heat up frying oil in a pan or set your deep fat fryer to 165C.

5. When the oil has reached temperature place the fattigman in the oil. They will float to the top so don't put too many in the pan/fryer at the same time. Turn them around so they're golden on both sides. Let them cool down, then dust with icing sugar on both sides.

## KOKOSMAKRONER

MAKES AROUND 30 COOKIES

Ingredients

- 8 egg whites
- 400 gr sugar / 2 cups / 14 oz
- 2 tsp vanilla sugar
- 400 gr dried coconut flakes / 4 cups / 13.6 oz

1. Pre-heat the oven to 180 C / 360 F / GM 4.

2. Whisk the egg whites in a big pan (off the heat) until you see small bubbles appear in the mixture.

3. Gently fold in the sugar, vanilla sugar and the dried coconut flakes.

4. Place the pan on a low heat and stir until the mixture turns gloopy and sticks to your spoon.

5. Take the pan off the heat and cover a baking sheet with parchment paper. Using a tablespoon place dollops of the

mixture onto the sheet and make sure to leave some space in between them.

6. Bake in the oven for 10 minutes, then let them cool down so they can set. By the time they're cold, they should be golden on the outside and white and gooey on the inside.

# AFTERWORD

I hope you've loved reading Northern Lights as much as I've loved writing it. If you've enjoyed this book, would you consider rating it and reviewing it on www.amazon.com? Reviews are very important to authors and I'd be really grateful!

## ACKNOWLEDGMENTS

Claire Jarrett, my editor, thank you for your passion and your dedication to making this novella the best it can be. I'm looking forward to having a Christmas drink with you and toasting to working on many more books together!

Thank you to my beta reader, Laure Dherbecourt, for being so thorough. I wish you an amazing Christmas on your tropical island :)

But most of all, thank you, my readers. Two years have passed since my dream of being a writer started coming to life. It's only because of your support and enthusiasm that I'm able to continue my writing journey. I wish you all a wonderful Christmas, and a fabulous 2019. Bring it on!

## ABOUT THE AUTHOR

Lise Gold is an author of lesbian fiction. Her romantic attitude, enthusiasm for travel and love for feel good stories form the heartland of her writing. Lise's novels are the result of a quest for a new passion, after spending fourteen years working as a designer. Lise lives in the UK with her wife.

## ALSO BY LISE GOLD

Lily's Fire

Beyond the Skyline

The Cruise

French Summer

Fireflies

Printed in Great Britain
by Amazon

66628265R00102